**The
Eleventh
Commandment**

**Other books
by Melville Shavelson**

HOW TO MAKE A JEWISH MOVIE
LUALDA
THE GREAT HOUDINIS!

The Eleventh Commandment

Melville Shavelson

READER'S DIGEST PRESS
Distributed by Thomas Y. Crowell Company
New York, 1977

Manufactured in the United States of America

LIBRARY OF CONGRESS CATALOGING IN PUBLICATION DATA

Shavelson, Melville, 1917–
   The eleventh commandment.

   I. Title.
PZ4.S53343E1   [PS3569.H357]   813'.5'4   77-23071
ISBN 0-88349-141-9

ISBN 0-88349-141-9

10 9 8 7 6 5 4 3 2 1

To Karin,
Amy, and Scott,

in the forlorn hope
that the world will grow up
when they do

ACKNOWLEDGMENT

The author wishes to acknowledge the existence of the state of Israel.

Preface

IT'S HARD to believe now that it ever happened. There are some who still insist it was a trick, a bluff, a carefully constructed pretense that no one dared challenge, the Emperor's New Clothes on Golda Meir, God forbid.

Henry Kissinger best expressed the world's relief when it was all over, after he had been called back into the Cabinet by a Carter administration completely confounded by the sudden shift in international relations and happy to have the blame taken by a Republican with a German accent. Dr. Kissinger told a relieved General Assembly of the United Nations, "The political and economic balance of the world has been restored to equilibrium because of Israel's overpowering adherence to the tradition of the Mosaic Law and its unwritten Eleventh Commandment."

There are some in this world, of course, who have never heard of this commandment. When Moses came down from Mount Sinai, he was too embarrassed to mention what God had carved, appropriately, into the back side of the Holy Tablets. It wasn't unwritten; it was unmentionable. The literal translation of what Jehovah engraved in fire is: "Thou Shalt Not Shtup a Shiksa." This admonition to refrain from sexual intercourse with Gentile females was couched by the Lord, in His infinite wisdom, in the vernacular most likely to be understood by those most likely to sin. They could not claim they did not understand His meaning. In the final reckoning, it was this, and this alone, that brought order back to a troubled planet.

The Lord is my shepherd, I shall not want; He leadeth me to lie down in green pastures, but only with a Nice Jewish Girl.

Order did return. In Israel itself the harems were broken up, and the dancing girls were banished to various kibbutzim, where they promptly opened massage parlors.

Golda Meir gave back her Rolls-Royce and Lear Jet and retired to private life once more, after her startling return to the office of prime minister at the height of the crisis. She did not open a massage parlor. As far as it is known.

Ronald Reagan revealed that he hadn't really been circumcised after all and was drummed out of his temple, smiling.

Only Jacob Schoenbaum, who had started the whole thing, was completely happy: He had saved his daughter Sonya's marriage and, only incidentally, the balance of power in the Middle East.

Contents

The same hands that shook ours so warmly only a few years back are now raised to denounce Zionism in the New York glass menagerie. The eyes are lowered, but the hands go up. They are the hands that applaud the assassin who climbs the speaker's dais waving an automatic olive branch with a loaded chamber, and the hands that write "racist" on the brow of the Nazis' victims.... Saddest of all in this bitter dispute is that there's really no difference in the political assessment of the two camps, only in the conclusions both draw from it: the doves hope that the Arabs will eventually resign themselves to our existence, while we *know* that they'll resign themselves to nothing short of our annihilation....

The solution? Look for it in the theatre of the absurd that is the world we live in.

—EPHRAIM KISHON, Israel's foremost humorist and conscience,
The Mark of Cain

1 Genesis

IT BEGAN, innocently enough, in Gracie Mansion. Mayor Abraham Beame was upstairs in his bedroom, taking a well-earned rest after an exhausting day of keeping the largest city in the world from teetering over the brink into bankruptcy. Downstairs, an outraged Jacob Schoenbaum was leading a group angrily protesting the mayor's action in removing their apartments from rent control. The two antagonists never met. No one could have foreseen then that the mayor's failure to awaken from his nap would trigger a series of events that would turn the world upside down. Archduke Francis Ferdinand at Sarajevo, Jacob Schoenbaum at Gracie Mansion—both caused explosions that would alter the history of mankind. The difference was that the archduke forgot to duck and had his head blown off, while Schoenbaum not only kept his head, but became the Messiah.

Gracie Mansion is an unlikely setting for an encounter that was to shake up the Geopolitik of the civilized world, meaning every country with a smog problem. It is a stylish, graceful home in a parklike setting on Manhattan's fashionable East Side. The city has crowded in on it, but its lawn and its trees have remained inviolate, immune to the skyrocketing tax rate because it is the official residence of New York City's mayor. It is the one refuge he can retreat to after the nerve-shattering experience of another day in office as the servant of a citizenry given to throwing beer bottles at umpires and Bronx cheers at the Mafia. It is a matter of historical record that three Presidents of the United States have been assassinated in office while no one has ever bothered to take a shot at New York's mayor. The job is punishment enough.

So it was no surprise to the mayor's harried secretary that another group of irate taxpayers had come to the mansion determined to face Abraham Beame with a personal grievance. It was a daily occurrence. The members of New York's Finest detailed to the mayor's protection would automatically give the leader of such a group a bored, professional bum's rush, on signal from the secretary. Had the secretary realized the formidable nature of his opponent on this brisk autumn evening, he might have hesitated. But it was his first encounter with Jacob Schoenbaum, and he made a fatal miscalculation.

On the surface, Schoenbaum, seven-five years old, looked like a nice little old Jewish gentleman. Inside the black alpaca overcoat with the worn fur collar, however, lived a tiger. The lined face was still strong; the chin was firm; the old eyes were aflame with righteous wrath. He stood out from the little group of protesters like Abraham Lincoln at a Ku Klux Klan rally. If Attila the Hun had been born Jewish, and with a little more chutzpa, he might have grown up to be Jacob Schoenbaum.

Raised amid the pushcarts of Orchard Street in a generation that had to fight its way to Hebrew school through streets whose turf belonged to Irishmen, Italians, Africans, and Chinese, Schoenbaum lived a childhood that made it easy for him to empathize, later, with little Israel's experiences in the United Nations. Like Israel, he chose to fight back, never giving an inch. His nose was bloodied on numerous occasions, his teeth were removed without benefit of dentistry, but his spirit had never been bruised. He learned at an early age to pry the loose cobblestones from the pavement and hurl them, with deadly accuracy, at the enemy. When attacked by a gang, he continued to battle back until battered into unconsciousness, and when his opponents, who were, after all, children, realized that his intent was to defend his honor to the death if necessary, they gave him a wide berth. What they could not face was reality. They wanted to humble him, but they were not willing to risk a murder rap to accomplish it. Even when only ten years old, Schoenbaum knew his most precious possession was his pride. Without it, he would rather die. With it, he was unconquerable.

When he grew up, unexpectedly in one piece, he carried the same attitude into the business world. Thus, he never became a rich man, even though he became a building contractor; he was too proud to pay anyone off. Consequently, he was visited often by the health department, the police department, and the fire department, who were not really interested in his health, his safety, or his inflammability. They were interested in getting him the hell out of business before his success jeopardized the system. His garbage was left uncollected; his traffic tickets escalated; his concrete-and-steel buildings were declared fire traps. He thrived on it. He fought back, he hollered, he insisted on rights they didn't know he had, he wrote to the newspapers, the Better Business Bureau, Walter Winchell, and he once telephoned President Franklin Delano Roosevelt at the White House, collect. It is a clue to Schoenbaum's personality that the call was accepted at a time when the nation was faced with the largest budget deficit in its history.

New York was his city. The beloved apartment where he lived in relative peace and happiness with his wife, Sophie, and his restless daughter, Sonya, was his Shangri-la, his Taj Majal. It took every penny of his retirement budget to meet the rent, but it was worth it. From this secure vantage point he could holler on the city, on its officials, on its mayor, on its noise and its dirt and its pollution, on its muggings and rapes and robberies, on everything that makes the island of Manhattan a prisoner of every union that can close one bridge, every mob that can shake down one trucking company, every prostitute who can parade openly on Broadway because she contributes to the Police Athletic League. Jacob Schoenbaum loved every scabrous inch of New York; it was his kind of town. Every day there was something new to holler on. It kept him young. Unlike his wife, Sophie, he had never thought seriously of leaving it.

Until today.

Schoenbaum had not come to Gracie Mansion to plead with the mayor on behalf of himself and his neighbors. Schoenbaum did not plead; Schoenbaum demanded. He recognized no authority but God's, and then only when He happened to agree with Schoenbaum.

He had already written the mayor, as spokesman for the neighborhood—Twenty-third Street and Lexington—about the terrible garbage collection, the dirty streets, and the fact that the bus did not stop at Twenty-third Street, only at Twenty-second. But age was beginning to tell. Before his rheumatism Schoenbaum would have willingly lain down in the gutter in front of the bus until it *did* stop at Twenty-third Street.

Now, at Gracie Mansion, he tried to reason first, presenting the group's complaint: Since the mayor had removed rent controls, those shlemiels, the landlords, had gotten together and raised the average rent from two hundred and fifty dollars a month to five hundred and fifty dollars. Was this democracy? Was this America? Would John Wayne do such a thing? For the group, for himself, Schoenbaum demanded justice: the landlords thrown in jail, rent control reimposed, and the linoleum fixed in the kitchen. Sophie had tripped twice. Otherwise, he was issuing a warning to Mayor Beame: Schoenbaum would be compelled to act.

The mayor's secretary concealed a smile and winked at the two policemen near his desk in the study on the first floor that was the mayor's office away from City Hall. So had Goliath smirked at David, before the rock hit him between the eyes. The secretary, a long-haired young man employed to show the administration's keen concern for the youth vote, made a note in the pad on his desk: "5:40 P.M. Nut."

"You got it down?" demanded Schoenbaum. "Also the linoleum?"

"I'll inform the mayor as soon as he gets up from his nap," said the secretary smoothly. He underlined the word "Nut."

"How can he sleep, the whole city is raising up the rent? I work all my life, the money in the bank means nothing, I got a daughter, for her I'd like a nice wedding, how can I afford? Wake him up."

"I'm very sorry, but—"

"Sure, he can sleep. Does *he* pay rent?"

"Mr. Schoenbaum, if you'll—"

"We all came here from Twenty-third Street, a long trip on the bus. I'm not a young man. Show a little respect. Wake him up, he'll thank you."

"And thank *you,* Mr. Schoenbaum; there are others waiting."

The young man signaled the two patrolmen. They took Schoenbaum by the elbows, not too gently.

"Let's go, Pop," said the first, urging him toward the door. Angrily and with unexpected strength, Schoenbaum shook himself free from their grasp.

He turned to the secretary again as the others watched. "Don't play games with Schoenbaum! Tell the mayor it's my last warning!"

He turned to the policemen. "Go ahead," he said, "throw

me out. You got pistols, shoot me. A nice job the mayor gives you. An old man, never did you any harm. Throw me out; break by me the leg; get your picture in the *Daily News!*''

Before they could stop him, he crossed to a wall of the office and pounded on it with his fist.

"Abraham Beame!" he shouted. "Wake up! It's later than you think!''

And then he was gone, swiftly, through the door, leaving the others behind. Schoenbaum never dragged out an exit.

Especially a good one.

On his way home alone in the bus, angry at the mayor's failure to give him an audience, Schoenbaum started drafting his battle plan. Like General Patton's, it would be unexpected, swift, and daring. It depended for its execution on a lightning thrust, raw courage, and Benjamin Ratner, pigeon. Ratner, an accountant with the Bell Telephone System, was a regular member of the pinochle-playing group that met for a pleasant, screaming altercation every Wednesday night in Schoenbaum's apartment. Most of the screaming was done by Ratner. Schoenbaum knocked him off so regularly it was a standing joke that the only reason Ratner showed up for the game was that he couldn't find a way to phone in the money. Schoenbaum knew that if he promised to allow Ratner to beat him one Wednesday night he could ask any favor within Ratner's power. Abraham Beame's doom was sealed.

Schoenbaum was already savoring his victory when his eye fell on a discarded newspaper on the seat next to him. He was momentarily distracted by the headlines: Saudi Arabia had purchased one hundred and sixty Tiger jets to combat the Mediterranean fruit fly; the United Nations was again condemning Israel, this time for not saving the stamps on a package that had exploded before being delivered to the prime minister.

Schoenbaum's anger at the world had one weak link: the tiny country established, against all reason, all hope, in a bleak desert in the geographical center of sixty million Arabs who didn't want it there. If Schoenbaum himself had chosen the spot, he couldn't have found one that would have antagonized more neighbors. He had watched over the years the struggle for survival, so nearly akin to his own, of the impossible nation with its impossible citizenry fighting impossible wars to impossible victories. Of course, he had never revealed his feelings; being Schoenbaum, he had to criticize every move, every bond drive, every Hadassah meeting his wife, Sophie, attended, but underneath, there was grudging admiration for Israel's lonely stand against a whole world determined to force it to lose its individuality, either by bombing it or by helping it. The bombs came with fuses, and the help came with strings; when you have Henry Kissinger for a friend, Schoenbaum was fond of paraphrasing, who needs an enemy? The nicest thing you could say about a Jewish boy who kissed the president of Egypt was that if his wife had been traveling with him, he wouldn't have had to.

It was Sophie's dream that when Sonya got married, Sophie and Schoenbaum would move to Israel to spend their declining years. It wouldn't be a simple matter to get Jacob to make the move, but Sophie had never had any real difficulty in twisting him around her little finger. First, she would tell him that in Israel nobody could fight City Hall since everybody in the government was Jewish, so why holler on them? This would wound Schoenbaum's pride; he felt he had the right to holler on anybody, Jew, Gentile, or Buddhist monk, who was not running things Schoenbaum's way. He was an equal-opportunity hollerer. Abraham Beame was Jewish, wasn't he? The challenge of an entire government made up of stubborn Jewish officials who would battle back on equal terms would be too enticing for Schoenbaum to resist. So they would go to Israel at his insistence, Sophie figured, and he would be busy and happy tilting at Jewish windmills, and Sophie would get a chance to do some shopping.

In her forty-three years of marriage, she hadn't had much opportunity. Schoenbaum had made a good living, but given his temperament, a great deal of it had gone for lawyers. The rest went for Sonya, their only child, who was beautiful and blond and claimed to be nineteen. Of course, Sonya had been nineteen for some time now, and people were starting to talk. If she didn't get married soon, she would be past the point of no return. But Sonya was of the new generation of liberated females. Most women with liberated ideas have lumpy bodies subordinated to brilliant minds; Sonya had a brilliant body and a lumpy mind. Her figure was designed for pleasure, soft and supple and roundly curved, constructed to drive Nice Jewish Boys insane. It was supplemented by a nature that can only be described politely as slightly overpassionate. And it's not that she wasn't intelligent; it was just that all the new ideas of female freedom had not yet been fully digested. Until she understood what it was all about, she preferred to allow herself complete abandon while she constructed her own code of ethics. This learning period made her extremely popular with the opposite sex, who were eager, nay, frantic, to assist in her education.

Schoenbaum, like most fathers, was completely unaware of Sonya's more earthy side. She was the only thing in the world in which he could find nothing to criticize. He loved Sonya with the unseeing eyes of a devoted parent who could not fathom how an old shlemiel like himself and a yenta like her mother could have brought into the world a creature as sweet and beautiful as their Sonya. In temple he would often give thanks to God and to Dr. Seymour Greenbaum, the surgeon who had bobbed her nose.

Of course, Schoenbaum had no intention of moving to Israel; the apartment, the city of New York, the battles with Sophie—those were his world. If Sonya got married and took up residence in the city, there would be even less reason to leave it. The thought of his perfect daughter gave him such a

feeling of warmth and content that he didn't even holler on the
bus driver for not stopping at Twenty-third Street. He got off at
Twenty-second and walked back toward the lovely apartment,
which that bum Abraham Beame was trying to wrest from
him, daydreaming of the moment Sonya would get married to
her handsome Orthodox millionaire doctor. It was the American Jewish Dream come true; Sophie had arranged it. She had
found a rich Park Avenue gynecologist who was unmarried
and happy about it and had sent Sonya to him for an examination. When he walked into the examining room, it was love at
first sight, at least for the doctor. The area in which he was a
specialist was also Sonya's. Nature took its unerring course,
and Sophie took hers. She advised Sonya from the sidelines,
like Woody Hayes coaching Ohio State, and the doctor was
overmatched from the outset. Sonya advanced; Sonya retreated; Sonya denied. The doctor still did not buy the ring,
although his panting could be heard all the way to Madison
Avenue. Finally, he invited Sonya up to his apartment and
plied her with Cuba Libres, which gives you an idea of his age.
It was the kickoff of the sexual Rose Bowl. Sonya remained
warm and loving and vertical, although the Coca-Cola was
making her sick. The doctor kept increasing the amount of
Ronrico rum in each drink, Sonya kept her dress tightly zip-
ped, and the doctor was going out of his mind for a glimpse of
what women usually paid him one hundred dollars an hour to
look at from a distance of three inches. In fact, he had seen all
of Sonya in that way several times in his office and knew her
geography thoroughly. Why, then, should he be going insane
for a peek? Obviously, the Lord has arranged things so that
gynecologists have short memories and long fuses; otherwise,
the race would die out. The upshot was that the doctor finally
proposed marriage and passed out simultaneously, as he had
been trying to keep up with Sonya and didn't realize she had
started to pour her Cuba Libres into his tank of tropical fish,
who were beginning to rumba.

Schoenbaum didn't know all these intimate details. Sophie had only told him the result: Their little Sonya was about to make the greatest catch of the matrimonial season; it was true love and a bank account at the Chase Manhattan that Sophie had thoroughly researched. Their cup of happiness was running over.

All this was flashing contentedly through Schoenbaum's mind as he turned the corner and saw the ambulance pulling away from the curb in front of the apartment house. The old man noted the shrieking of the siren and determined to write a letter to Mount Sinai—what kind of therapy is a geshrei like that, someone is sick inside, all this noise to get them to a hospital where everybody walks on tiptoe? And then he saw Sonya in the street, and there were tears in her eyes, and some of the neighbors who always played the television so loud they should drop dead were with her, and it occurred to Schoenbaum that his wife, Sophie, wasn't.

Sonya turned when she saw her father and ran to him, like a child, because she needed his strength.

"Papa!" she cried, and put her arms around him. The Last Angry Man, she called him to her friends, but there are moments when anger is necessary. She was ashamed, sometimes, when he wrote letters to the newspapers complaining about taxes, about crime, about television, about the President, about the Pope—he felt it was inconsistent for the Pontiff to be against both abortion and divorce: "If he would allow one, they wouldn't need the other. Why can't the shlimazl see this?" When that had appeared in the *Post*, over her father's signature, she had avoided her friends for days. But now the sight of his small, indomitable figure was as welcome as a spring rain. She needed someone to holler on God.

"Papa," she said again, "they've taken Mama to the hospital—it's my fault, all my fault!"

"What are you talking? You hit her?"

"Worse. I told her the wedding is off."

"The Orthodox doctor? He doesn't want to marry you?"

"No, Papa." How could she make him understand? "*I* don't want to marry *him*."

"Listen, it's not so terrible. We'll find you another doctor. You know how many graduate each year?"

"Papa, you don't understand. I want to be a free soul. I don't want to marry anybody. Especially a doctor. Ever. But that doesn't mean I don't want to live with a man. Until we get tired of each other."

"Holler," said Schoenbaum, "maybe we can get the ambulance to come back. I feel a little dizzy."

2 Schoenbaum's Appointment in Samarra

THE FATEFUL MEETING of the OPEC foreign ministers was held, this time, in Cairo itself. Thus, if there were a repetition of the Vienna raid and they all were captured, the terrorists wouldn't have to demand a plane to fly them all the way back to the Arab world before releasing them, and a great deal of aviation fuel would be saved. None of the ministers could figure out why Arabs had kidnapped their own people in the first place, until they realized the PLO hadn't hijacked a plane for a long time and probably wanted to see the movie.

The gathering at the Nile Hilton exuded confidence. Several sheikhs from the coastal sultanates brought along entire harems, so their wives could go shopping without worrying about the old man, stuck in the hotel with nothing to do. But the real business of the conference was conducted in the suite of Colonel Muammar el-Qaddafi, the young Libyan firebrand, meeting with the boys from Saudi Arabia and Syria and Jordan and Egypt and making the fateful decision that was to bring them on a collision course with Schoenbaum.

"Our plan is working," Qaddafi told them. "It's the old trick of hitting someone over the head with a hammer; it feels so good when you stop. Every time we raise the price of oil only fifteen percent we get a nice pat on the back from *Time* magazine. If we raise the price only ten percent, we get the cover. Of course, we only raise our prices because of the inflation in the West. We haven't yet figured out what causes this inflation, but it is suspicious that every time we raise oil prices inflation seems to increase. It should be obvious there is a plot here, and that Israel is behind it. More and more, the West is beginning to recognize who is their true enemy. The government of Israel has not yet sent Washington one drop of oil to prove their alleged friendship. Halvah yes, oil no. The United States' economy is grinding to a halt, and Israel will not lift a finger to help. It shatters one's faith in human nature."

He shook his head, sadly. King Khalid of Saudi Arabia, the kindly old man who had risen to the throne of his country by dint of good deeds, love of his people, and the fact that somebody knocked off his brother, put it into words for the others. "Listen, Muammar," he said, "you think we should squeeze quite so hard? Somebody's liable to get mad. Also, those votes in the United Nations are getting a little ridiculous. Shouldn't we let Israel get one or two little African votes? I mean, Nick the Greek won't even quote a point spread any more."

Those were not his precise words in Arabic, but they do convey the sense of his concern.

"Nonsense," shouted Qaddafi, not a man to be persuaded by pity. "There's nothing to worry about! When we first started raising prices, everybody said the traffic jams in the West would come to an end, the autobahns would be empty. Look what's happened. They're buying more of our oil than ever before. Accidents on the Los Angeles freeway are up a healthy twenty percent. Western man will give up his home, his family, and, finally, his mistress, before he will put his Camaro up on blocks. We've barely scratched the surface. The time has come to activate Plans A and B!''

There was a murmur from the others. This was it. Kismet. The moment had finally arrived. They all knew, of course, what Qaddafi was hinting at. Plan A was simplicity itself: an acceleration of the price squeeze that would, eventually, transform Western civilization into the Sahara and the Arab world into the French Riviera. Amman was to become Paris, and Beverly Hills would be Sharm-el-Sheikh.

That, of course, would take a long time. But once this meeting's new, massive increases in the price of oil were announced, the resultant outcry from the West would be so loud, the fear of losing their Camaros so deep, they would hardly notice that the tanks and guns they had been selling to buy gas for their cars were being quietly assembled in the Sinai and near the Golan Heights. Plan B would be put in operation.

Plan B was even more simple than Plan A. It was to be the last battle.

Having sworn each other to secrecy, the oil ministers broke up the meeting in high spirits and descended to the lobby of the Nile Hilton. The Iranian foreign minister, passing the newsstand, idly picked up a copy of the air edition of the New York *Times*. He wanted, of course, to check on his country's holdings in the stock market, which included a page and a half of the listings. It never occurred to him to turn to the next page, the classified section. For in that very edition appeared Schoenbaum's riposte to Mayor Abraham Beame that was to help undo everything that had been decided that day in the Nile Hilton's King Tut Suite.

Jacob Schoenbaum, like fate, had an appointment in Samarra.

3 Sonya Does It Because She Enjoys

THE FIRST FEW days no one was allowed to visit Sophie Schoenbaum in the hospital, and she felt it was a good thing. How could she face the terrible old man she had loved so deeply for so long when she was about to ruin all his careful plans? What good was the precious apartment now if she was gone and Schoenbaum was to be alone? Sonya couldn't cook; Sonya didn't clean; Sonya had already announced, on that fateful afternoon, that she was leaving. She was going to live with a fellow in Greenwich Village, some nudnik who sold leather belts on the sidewalk on Eighth Street. The world was upside down, women wanted to be men, and men wanted to be bachelors. The magazines were full of naked pictures, and girls were doing it twice as often as before because the young people wanted zero population growth. Nothing made sense. If you were on welfare, the government paid for your abortion, but only if you weren't married. In school they taught everything but how to preserve virginity. It was becoming a lost art, like stained glass.

It had been different when Sophie was growing up. If you were a Nice Jewish Girl and allowed a fellow to put his hands on your knee, instantly you became pregnant. If he touched you a little higher up, twins. Of course, he had to be Jewish. If he were a shaygitz, one touch, white slavery. It was a harmless enough mythology, most girls didn't believe it, and it led to a certain amount of consumer research; but it was a reflection of the spirit of the age. All American wars were just; all sex was dirty; all Presidents were honest; all Negroes were happy; all wives did it because their husbands forced them. Why Negro wives were happy if their husbands were forcing them, no one ever figured out. If you brought it up, you were a Communist.

So life had been comfortably circumscribed if you were a girl from a good Jewish family going to NYU. The only trouble with NYU was that it had a campus near Washington Square, and Washington Square was full of troublemakers and anarchists. One day Sophie had met a fellow making a speech that was so angry, so impassioned, so much against everything that existed in the world that Sophie felt it necessary to wait for him to finish and ask him what he was *for?*

"What kind cockamamy question is *this?*" shouted the young Schoenbaum in his normal tone of voice. "Why do I have to be *for* anything?"

"There must be something you like."

"Trotsky, I like. Pastrami, I like. That's all. In this world, that's a pretty good average."

"How about girls?"

"I never had time to find out. But you want my opinion, the odds are against it."

The next day Sophie was standing in the same spot, he was making the same speech. And the next. She found out he was a carpenter, an electrician, an immigrant. He found out she came from West End Avenue, beyond the pale. He got angry at her for coming from West End Avenue. One evening, when he had finished making a speech, they sat down together on a park bench and argued some more. Schoenbaum put a hand on her knee.

"My mother says you can get pregnant from that," Sophie told him.

"What kind of stupid mother you got?" he shouted. "Frightening a girl like this? Fairy tales!" He put a hand on her other knee. "All right," he said. "Now I'll have to marry you or you'll have twins."

She kissed him, and the odds against girls changed.

Her family had been outraged. "A nothing!" they told her. "An agitator! A radical! Emma Goldman he should have married, not you; it'll never work!"

It had worked for forty-three years, Sophie thought as the nurse took her pulse again, still with the worried look. It's all right, Sophie wanted to say to her, I know what's wrong with my heart. Listen, it hasn't been a bad forty-three years; Schoenbaum always found something to holler on; always life was being examined in our house; all the things that should be put right in the world were in Schoenbaum's department; he never shirked. It wasn't easy being married to him, but it was never dull. Who could say more?

She knew, of course, that he had gone to Gracie Mansion to do battle with the mayor of New York on the day she had been admitted to Mount Sinai Hospital. When she read in the *Times* that Abraham Beame was going to make a statement on television answering critics of his rent control policies, she had a feeling it had something to do with Schoenbaum. She asked the nurse to turn on the television. Sophie hadn't been allowed to talk on the telephone or to watch the television set because the doctor believed the excitement might be too much for her, and the nurse at first demurred. Sophie had trained under the master. She demanded the television should be turned on. If she died from boredom, how would it look on the chart?

Schoenbaum, of course, prevented from seeing Sophie by the doctor, who knew him too well, had been like a caged lion.

An old, caged lion in a black alpaca overcoat with a worn fur collar. To keep sanity, he had concentrated on *L'Affaire* Abraham Beame. Two days after his battle at Gracie Mansion he placed the advertisement in the New York *Times* classified section that was to become famous: "FOR RENT: Town house, E. Side. Furn. 6 b.r., 5 baths, svts qtrs. $200 mo. BU 8-0604 day or nite."

A furious mayor tried to find out who had given out the unlisted number of the hot line beside his bed in Gracie Mansion which was ringing off the hook, day and nite. He got no place. The New York *Times* stood on its constitutional rights to protect its sources. Besides, the *Times* hadn't really cared for any mayor of New York since Peter Stuyvesant. The Bell Telephone Company swore it had no clue. They didn't know about Benjamin Ratner, accountant and pigeon, who had grabbed a fast peek at the unlisted numbers file and would soon be winning, regularly, at pinochle. The mayor couldn't nap, he couldn't sleep, and he didn't connect the incident with the little old man who had come to Gracie Mansion with a protest, because Beame hadn't had the courtesy to wake up.

The matter might have rested there had not Schoenbaum, flushed with victory, overplayed his hand. After seeing Abraham Beame looking pale and sleepless in the televised interview from his official residence, during which a phone kept ringing continuously in the background and the mayor kept twitching, Schoenbaum sent him a wire: TAKE DOWN THE RENT. REMEMBER PHARAOH, FIVE MORE PLAGUES TO COME. SCHOENBAUM.

It was an indiscretion. The long-haired secretary had a good memory; the name struck a bell, albeit a cracked one. He found his notation: "5:40 P.M. *Nut.*" There was a record of the group of protesters and, most important of all, the addresses. The battle was joined, the City of New York v. Jacob Schoenbaum, Giant Killer.

It hadn't been a good idea for Sophie to watch the mayor on

television. She recognized at once the practiced hand of the old man she loved, the Jewish St. George, Don Quixote of Twenty-third and Lexington, in every twitch of the mayor of the greatest city in the world. The lifting of rent controls, he shouted, was an absolute necessity in this age of inflation. Any citizen who attempted to intimidate the mayor would feel the full weight of the city's power on his unbending neck! The mayor was so furious Sophie knew her fiery husband was somehow at the bottom of it all. She felt this was a milestone; Schoenbaum had gone too far, and she would not be around to protect him from himself. She informed the doctor she must see her husband at once.

When Schoenbaum heard that Sophie had asked to see him, he had a premonition. Suddenly the struggle against the city didn't seem important. Forty-three years of hollering on the same person had led to a beautiful relationship that Schoenbaum didn't want to see disappear, not this way.

On the way to the hospital he stopped and bought a dozen roses. He had meant to buy Sophie roses the night of their marriage, but instead, he had taken her to see Joe Louis knock out Max Baer. Only now did it occur to him she might not have enjoyed it any more than Max Baer did.

When he walked into the hospital room, Sophie was sitting up in bed weakly, putting on lipstick. Like always, Jacob thought. A woman's face could fall apart, color the lips, who'll notice? Didn't she know it only made her look twice as pale?

She saw the roses.

"I'm that sick?" were her first words.

"What are you talking? I can't bring flowers? There's a law?"

"Shhh, we're in a hospital."

"By the city it's a hospital. In the Catskills they wouldn't give a room this small to a Reformed rabbi."

"Listen, Schoenbaum," Sophie said, and she realized she

wasn't hollering, but she couldn't help it, he looked so help-less, fumbling about for something to put the flowers in, too proud to call the nurse, finally throwing out the bouquet from the Haddassah and substituting his own, grumbling all the while. "I want you to know something. All the time I hollered at you, I only hollered because I cared."

Schoenbaum looked up, startled, shocked, almost dropping the vase.

"You're *that* sick?" he asked.

They both knew then. He sat down beside the bed and took her hand.

"Listen," he told her, "I don't want you should be upset; they're tearing down the building."

"What building?"

"What building is there? The one with our apartment. The whole building. The city says it's unsafe; the mayor says it's condemned; with the landlord it's all right. In the new building he can raise up the rent again, buy a Mercedes. Four-door."

My God, thought Sophie. To lose his wife and his apartment at one time. Also, perhaps, his daughter. What would he have left? The alpaca overcoat with the awful fur collar? Her heart bled for him.

"Schoenbaum," she whispered, "remember how I wanted to go to live in Isreal after Sonya got married, and you didn't want to?"

"You want to go, we'll go," Schoenbaum said.

He had never given in to her before this easily. She had to speak carefully to keep her voice from breaking.

"Not me," she said. "You. You and Sonya. And quickly."

"But she's not married yet! She says she's not getting mar-ried ever. She wants to be up to date."

"She told you about this belt peddler, in Greenwich Vil-lage, the one she's in love with?"

Schoenbaum nodded, grieved. "Some love," he said. "No wedding, no rabbi, just monkey business."

"It's a new world. The Nussbaums' Gloria, for three years she's living with a taxi driver. It's not even his own cab."

"We've lived too long," her husband said. "To see this. Shiksas I could understand, but Nice Jewish Girls?"

"I never wanted to tell you about Sonya," Sophie told him. "I didn't want you to holler on her, too. It's been going on with her a long time."

Schoenbaum lit up one of his favorite cigars, Manuelo y Vega, Havana. Illegal. For Schoenbaum that made them sweeter.

"Sophie," he said finally, "our little Sonya is a nafka? Is this what you're telling?"

"No, no, thank God. A nafka does it for money; Sonya does it because she enjoys. It's the latest thing for women, enjoying."

"She's not pregnant from too much enjoying?"

"No, the girls today, they're careful."

Schoenbaum sighed, his universe crumbling.

"It must take a lot of careful," he said. He couldn't quite understand. In his world, in his generation, the thrill lay in the wonder, the surprise, the inaccessibility of femininity. How could it be that in this day and age smorgasbord had taken the place of a la carte? How could it be better, for anyone? Especially his lovely daughter?

The nurse interrupted them then, giving Sophie some pills and ordering her to lie down. She tried ordering Schoenbaum to leave and to put out his awful cigar, but something in his face told her it wouldn't do any good. After all, she told herself, what difference did it make now? She had seen the chart. She left.

After the door closed, Schoenbaum sat silently, looking at the window, at the lights of the city through the window, listening to his wife's heavy breathing. Fourteen thousand six hundred nights he had lain beside her, listening to that breathing; he had figured it out once on the little calculator, fourteen thousand six hundred, it must be up to over fifteen thousand now; it still annoyed him. Only tonight not so much as usual.

Finally, he turned to her. "Tell me," he said, "did you ever?"

"Ever what?"

"Enjoy?"

"Twice," Sophie said.

"In forty-three years, twice?"

"So maybe three times. I got a bad memory."

"*That* you would remember," he said, and saw she was smiling at him, and it hurt him. He couldn't remember the last time they had smiled together. He should have been kinder to her, he should have been more like other husbands, told her openly how much he loved her; but he was Schoenbaum, so he couldn't. And she had understood, which made him feel terrible, and still he couldn't bring himself to say it. He looked at her now and hoped she would see his eyes were saying what his lips could not.

She saw.

"Schoenbaum," she said, and her voice was urgent, "this time listen, don't argue. The apartment is gone; anyway, you couldn't afford the rent now; forget it. Go to Israel. Take Sonya. Watch over her. Believe me, it won't be simple. Get her married. In Israel they do the impossible."

"It sounds to me," Schoenbaum said, "Entebbe was easier."

"And the wedding should be in the house, with friends, with flowers, with food, not in a synagogue. Do this for me."

Schoenbaum leaned over and kissed his wife. "Don't worry," he said, "I'll do it."

She smiled again now, at peace. When Schoenbaum gave his word, it was done.

4 Exodus

THE LIGHTS of the Promised Land gleamed below the huge El Al 747 as it circled over Tel Aviv in the landing pattern for Ben-Gurion, née Lydda, Airport. The name had been changed *after* David Ben-Gurion was dead and buried, none of his countrymen wanting to give him the satisfaction while he was alive. After all, he had almost single-handedly created the country, and they had rewarded him by throwing him out of the government, kicking him out of the party he had founded, and sending him to live in the Negev Desert.

They didn't want to spoil him.

Ben-Gurion, being the first Israeli, understood completely. It was love. He had responded in kind. He deliberately destroyed his own administration because he hated one of his Cabinet ministers and couldn't stand him around. The Lavon Affair, they called it, and Ben-Gurion had devoted his administration to attacking Pinhas Lavon as a spy, a traitor, and a shlemiel, which put him one up on Gamal Abdul Nasser. Then Ben-Gurion retired to Kibbutz Sde Boker and took his phone off the hook. When the country needed him, the government had to travel down to the middle of the desert and beg him to come back and show them how to win another war. After he showed them, they sent him back to the desert, and he took his phone off the hook again.

It was a country designed for Schoenbaum.

He stared out the plane's window at the lights; so many tall buildings, so many hotels along the shore of the Mediterranean. This is what they did with the money I gave for Israel Bonds? Schoenbaum asked himself. I wrote on the check it should be for tanks, for barbed wire; instead, they built Miami Beach! He sighed, contentedly. He hadn't even landed, already he was fighting City Hall.

Seated next to him, Sonya wondered how she had ever let her father talk her into leaving New York. Of course, she had finally broken up with Bernie, her Greenwich Village admirer, after he began using his hand-crafted leather belts on her. *That* liberated she was not. In fact, if truth were known, Sonya was not much different from the girls of her mother's generation, who danced to the music of Glen Gray and his Casa Loma Orchestra and secretly longed to be attacked by Errol Flynn on his yacht, but were afraid of getting seasick. The difference was that Sonya's generation was not afraid of getting seasick or anything else. What was gone was not virginity, but sham. The honesty that brought about Watergate and the end of the Vietnam War made it possible for girls to live openly the fantasies they had only whispered about before, and the result was a healthier and more normal world. Girls were not only reading *Fanny Hill,* but writing it and living it. Sonya had attended Sarah Lawrence College in New York, a school for the elite that had become a fountainhead of the movement for women's rights. It had opened her eyes. That blacks had been oppressed and deprived in American society had always been obvious; that women had been segregated sexually had never seriously occurred to her. Sonya had broken out of the bonds of puritanism with so much enthusiasm that she had become the most popular date on campus. After graduation, she had felt the urge for a period of experimentation before settling into the married state. She had reluctantly gone along with her mother's campaign for the Park Avenue doctor until it became serious; then she had escaped. After graduation, she had also decided on a career as a professional writer as an indication of her liberated status. It had a nice ring to it, and while she was in bed with a young man, she could always claim she was thinking. Jacqueline Susann had undoubtedly started the same way.

In Sophie's time, a girl often married because it was the only socially acceptable outlet for her suppressed sexuality and energy. Today men and their appetites and abilities are openly discussed in magazines edited by and for women. Joe Namath's formerly hidden charms are now stapled to the centerfolds of these magazines for any girl to see and evaluate. Today's feminine graduate prepares to choose a mate and/or a career on a basis far sturdier than ignorance. Perhaps, again, the main difference with Sophie's generation is that it is now fashionable to tell the truth.

In the villages of Sicily, to this day, it is the custom of the parents of the bride to parade the bloodstained sheets of the honeymoon bed around the village square, to prove proudly to the community their daughter's innocence on her wedding night. However, since the advent of the automobile, television, and Gloria Steinem, it has become more and more necessary to substitute the blood of a chicken. Only the chickens are in favor of returning to the old days. The old people themselves merely shrug. For centuries, everybody knew the girls always took a chicken to the bed; what hot-blooded Sicilian male would wait until the marriage night? The difference today is that it is done openly; the honeymoon couple dines on chicken soup.

In spite of all this, Sonya knew that someday she would

want to experience something more lasting than a fleeting pleasure; she would want to feel the earth move. The problem with the new freedom for women was the freedom it gave to men, exactly the one they had been seeking all the time. "Love 'em and leave 'em," as it had once been euphemistically known, now had become modernized to "Drill 'em and dump 'em." Somewhere, Sonya had once heard an old recording of Hoagy Carmichael's "Stardust":

> Sometimes I wonder why I spend the lonely night
> Dreaming of a song
> Its melody haunts my reverie
> And I am once again with you
> When our love was new
> And each kiss an inspiration. . . .

Somehow, after that "Drill 'em and dump 'em" sounded flat. So when Bernie the Belter practiced the new philosophy on her, she had burst into tears, grabbed up her faded jeans, her Hare Krishna sweat shirt, her worn sandals, and her Saks Fifth Avenue charge card, and left him. She knew it wasn't Bernie's fault. He was just keeping up with the Joneses. All the men in the New York crowd had leaped on the new credo with the same enthusiasm.

When her father suggested she accompany him to Israel, Sonya at first cried, then she fought, then she hollered, and, finally, she thought about it. She wanted to get out of New York. In a new country, a pioneer society, a land with new values, perhaps she'd find a different kind of man, and the earth would move for both of them. And the search might give a new lift to her writing career, which up until then had been limited to buying a typewriter ribbon.

She allowed Schoenbaum to believe she was doing it for him. It was time, she said, for her father to get away from the city that had so many old memories and old enemies, to a land where he could start all over, making new enemies. She had smiled at him then, and Schoenbaum felt the hurt in his heart subsiding. Perhaps she was still his Sonya, the child who had run to him when he had come home at night from hollering at the office, to kiss him and see him pretend he hated such open affection, and sometimes she hadn't run to him, and laughed when she saw the sudden hurt in his eyes, and then made it up to him twice over.

They got off the plane at Ben-Gurion Airport and were loaded into a bus that took them to the customs area. It was hot, crowded, noisy. This was the Middle East; Schoenbaum and Sonya found themselves wondering if the very spot they were standing on had been the one where the last bomb had gone off, the last machine gun had splattered its deadly rounds into the walls. When they had left Kennedy Airport in New York, the security check had been the most thorough they had ever experienced because their destination was Tel Aviv. Twice every bit of luggage had been opened and sifted through, dogs had been called in to sniff for plastic explosives, and then, the final indignity, each had been subjected to a thorough frisking by experienced security hands.

"What's the matter?" Schoenbaum had demanded characteristically. "To you I look like an Arab? An old man, you got to feel his pupik? If you find anything, let me know, it'll be a nice surprise."

"Papa, shhhh!" Sonya had whispered. "Remember, it's for Israel."

She had said the magic word. Schoenbaum had subsided, feeling guiltily that perhaps by protecting his pupik he had been aiding King Hussein. Now, at Ben-Gurion Airport, here in the eye of the hurricane, a Jewish customs officer waved them through without examining their baggage. Schoenbaum stopped short.

"You're not going to look in the valise?" he inquired.

"Shalom," said the officer. "You are our guest."

"Could be dynamite, bombs, marijuana!"

"Papa!" Sonya cautioned.

"Pass," said the officer.

"No," said Schoenbaum. "Open the valise, at least look. I could be also a fedayeen."

"You're an old man."

"Look what they can do with makeup. Did you see perhaps *King Kong?*"

"Pass," insisted the officer.

"Papa!" pleaded Sonya again.

"I wouldn't feel safe in such a country, they don't open up the valise. Open up the valise! No wonder it happened on Yom Kippur!"

Without another word, the customs officer, a nice young man with a fine build, Sonya noted, grabbed one of Schoenbaum's bags from the cart, lifted it on the table, opened it up, and rifled through it with practiced hands. He brought out four boxes of Manuelo y Vega cigars.

"You are allowed only one hundred cigars," he said, placing the boxes to one side. "Confiscated."

"Cigars?" shouted Schoenbaum. "You got maybe a war here, people are shooting at you with cigars? Give back the boxes; you know how much it costs, Havana?"

"Please," said Sonya to the officer. "My father is an old man. It's the only pleasure he has left."

"I also give to the UJA," Schoenbaum reminded him.

The officer looked at Sonya for the first time. His eyes widened in approval.

"For you, I'll do it," he said. "It's not the only pleasure *I've* got left." And he winked.

My God, Sonya thought, I never left New York. But she smiled at him; for Schoenbaum's sake, she told herself.

"What hotel are you staying at?" inquired the customs officer, putting the cigar boxes back in the valise.

"The Waldorf," Sonya told him. He was quite a handsome young man.

"Only until we get an apartment," Schoenbaum insisted. "We're here permanent."

"You want my advice?" the customs officer said. "Forget

about an apartment. Call my Uncle Zvi; he's got a real estate business on Dizengoff. You should buy yourself a house. You can't believe the rents they're getting here; the mayor took off rent control.''

''Does the mayor have a private phone?'' Schoenbaum asked thoughtfully, taking Uncle Zvi's business card.

''Papa!'' Sonya warned. ''Not again. We'll run out of countries.''

''May I have your passports?'' asked the customs officer.

''What for?'' demanded Schoenbaum. ''You're also Immigration?''

''No, I just wanted to find out your daughter's name.'' He grinned. He had a nice smile.

''Sonya Schoenbaum,'' said Sonya. ''The passport won't be necessary.'' Why should he look at the passport and learn her age? Even her father couldn't remember how long she had been nineteen.

''My name is Chaim Barak,'' said the customs officer. ''Only it used to be Harold Bernstein. I'm from Dallas.''

''You got a good football team, Chaim,'' said Schoenbaum, who watched every Monday night.

''Not anymore. I live in Petach Tikva now, near Tel Aviv. Nobody in Petach Tikva has ever seen a pigskin.''

''Could somebody else pass by before Rosh Hashonah?'' asked a loud voice, and Sonya looked up, surprised to see the line of passengers waiting impatiently to get through the barrier. Watching Chaim-Harold, she hadn't been conscious of anyone else.

Schoenbaum had turned at the interruption. ''You own maybe the airport?'' he inquired of the irate man behind him. He hadn't had a good argument for thirty seconds.

''Papa, come on,'' urged Sonya as Chaim-Harold handed back the valise with the precious cigars inside. ''We have to get a taxi for the hotel.''

''You won't get one this time of day,'' Harold told her, unwilling to see her leave. ''If you do, they'll rob you.''

"Rosh Hashonah?" said another voice behind Schoenbaum. "We'll be lucky if we get through here before they start the next war."

"If you wait half an hour," Chaim insisted, "I'll be off duty. I'll drive you."

Schoenbaum's radar, which had been dormant, suddenly focused on what was going on between Sonya and Harold. The signals had been picked up by half the passengers in line, but Schoenbaum had been so interested in his cigars he hadn't noticed.

"We'll take a taxi, let them rob," he announced, taking Sonya's arm. Who needed a customs officer in the family? For his Sonya, Schoenbaum meant to investigate if Abba Eban had money.

"Shalom," said Sonya to Harold, who was breathing hard.

"Shalom means 'Peace,'" he said, eyeing her figure and smiling again.

"Shalom, shalom," said Sonya, and smiled back. They had nice Customs in this country.

The Waldorf-Astoria Hotel in Tel Aviv has little in common with its New York City namesake. The one in New York doesn't have even one mikvah, while the Waldorf in Tel Aviv has two, His and Hers. The mikvah, of course, is the ritual bath whose origins are lost in religious antiquity. Its cleansing powers are deemed to be divine, but since the one at the Waldorf used ordinary Tel Aviv tap water, which has on occasion been refused by thirsty camels after a thirty-day trek across the Negev, God has His work cut out for Him. In the dining room the hotel uses bottled water, figuring the Lord would be too tired to bother after purifying the water in the mikvah.

Schoenbaum and Sonya arrived at the hotel after a lengthy argument with the taxi driver. Schoenbaum, who had never been in Israel before, insisted the driver was taking the long way around, to run up the meter. The driver told him the long way around was through Lebanon, he wouldn't be such an idiot. Schoenbaum compromised by paying the fare and withholding the tip. The driver advised Schoenbaum to look both ways carefully before crossing any street in Tel Aviv in the future, as he had four brothers also driving cabs, and rattled away in his taxi, leaving Schoenbaum outraged but reinvigorated.

However, since the Waldorf-Astoria elevators didn't run on Shabbat, the Sabbath, Schoenbaum and Sonya had to stagger up four flights of stairs with their baggage, since the only bellboy was Orthodox. By that time they both were exhausted. Their rooms, two adjoining singles with a fine view of the municipal swimming pool, were comfortable by Israeli standards, and Schoenbaum was soon in his bed. He was awakened by the telephone ringing. He picked it up.

"A person can't sleep?" he inquired.

"Operator," said a voice.

"Who's calling?" Schoenbaum demanded.

"This is the hotel operator."

"You want something?"

"No. *You* want something?"

"What would I want? I was asleep!" shouted Schoenbaum, for the first time feeling a touch of sympathy for Abraham Beame.

"Listen, don't holler on me," said the operator, who was a nice old lady with a sense of power. "I didn't ring; who would want to talk to such a nudnik, gets angry over nothing? Next door I rang the phone; is it my fault the walls are shmattas?" She switched to another call. "Waldorf-Astoria," she said. "East, believe me."

The sound of Sonya's voice through the wall caused Schoenbaum's anger to subside.

The operator was right. The walls were shmattas. The telephone had rung next door. Sonya was laughing, a warm, intimate laugh he had never heard before.

"No, I'm not tired," she was saying. "A nightclub? Good heavens, they have nightclubs in the Holy Land? . . . What else do they have?" She laughed again. "Now, now, you're getting biblical. . . . No, don't worry, he's dead to the world. Go ahead. Make a reservation."

"Make it for three," called Schoenbaum.

"Oh, my God!" said Sonya. "The walls are shmattas."

"You heard? I'm going with you."

"Papa, shh, Chaim can hear you!"

"In that case, shalom, Chaim, I promised her mother, no monkey business until she gets married."

"Papa!"

"So a nightclub is a bad idea; that's where monkey business starts. Call up your Uncle Zvi; we'll go look at houses. . . . Chaim? You hear?"

"He hears, he hears," said Sonya wearily. "He says how can you look at houses in the middle of the night?"

"By New York time, it's early. I'm on New York time. His Uncle Zvi's in real estate, he's also on New York time."

"It's no use," Sonya whispered into the telephone. "We'll have to make it a double date with your Uncle Zvi. Tomorrow night I'll make it up to you, I promise."

"Over my dead body," said Schoenbaum. "Remember, the walls are shmattas."

The evening was a disaster as far as Chaim was concerned. Schoenbaum insisted on sitting in the front seat so he could see. Sonya sat in the back of the car with Uncle Zvi, whose real name turned out to be Sam and who spoke with a Texas drawl. He explained it was the policy in Israel to adopt Hebrew names. Actually, when Chaim lived in Dallas, his name had been Harold Bernstein because very few boys in Dallas are named Chaim. Very few are named Harold Bernstein either, which is one reason the family moved to Israel.

Uncle Zvi was a large man who wore a ten-gallon hat and

Levi's. If it was good enough for Lyndon Johnson, it was good enough for him, he explained when necessary, which was often. He had become a legendary figure around Tel Aviv because he thought big. As a Texan he couldn't understand a real estate deal for less than ten thousand acres. If you had ten thousand acres in Israel, the north forty would be in Damascus. Consequently, he never drove a hard bargain over what he considered a pea patch. Since that covered almost every lot he had for sale, he was at the mercy of all those who did drive a hard bargain, meaning everyone in Israel without a ten-gallon hat.

The ride turned out to be a joint fishing expedition: Uncle Zvi was trying to determine how much money Schoenbaum had, Schoenbaum was trying to determine how much money Chaim-Harold had, Sonya was trying to determine how they could ditch the two old men, and Chaim-Harold was trying to determine how far Sonya went on a first date.

Under Schoenbaum's careful probing, Harold revealed he was really a doctor. Not a completely satisfactory doctor, because he had a PhD from Texas Tech, not an MD from Johns Hopkins. His doctorate was in geology, and in Dallas he had worked for Texaco as a seismologist. What this meant, Uncle Zvi explained, was that Harold was a Doctor of Oil.

"So how come he's got a job arresting cigars?" Schoenbaum wanted to know, still hurting over the treatment of his Manuelo y Vegas.

"When I came here," Chaim-Harold explained, "I didn't realize the one thing Israel didn't have was oil, and what she had too much of was PhDs. So I took an examination for the Customs Service, and I got the job because nobody was taking that examination anymore. So many customs inspectors got shot up at the airport, they were all volunteering for the Golan Heights."

"You must be very brave," Sonya said admiringly from the back seat, "and the work must be simply fascinating."

Chaim-Harold turned around to look at her. Sonya was leaning forward, and the full charge of her voluptuous figure hit him with the effect of a Molotov cocktail. He swallowed hard once or twice and brushed two pedestrians and a Volkswagen into the curb before he recovered from her cleavage.

"Fascinating, my ass," he said, hoping his choice of language would get her mind back to fundamentals. "I could get blown up; I could get wounded; I could get knifed in the back. Who knows, this could be my last night on earth. I wish we could do something together to make it memorable."

"I have a feeling we will," Sonya said breathlessly, and Chaim brushed another unwary pedestrian into the gutter.

Schoenbaum was eyeing the two young people unhappily. Monkey business, he thought. Next thing they'll move in together and live happily ever after behind the baggage, without a rabbi. What a world. And in addition to all this, none of the houses Uncle Zvi had pointed out to him were anywhere within his means. The tiniest house with any sort of lawn had spiraled astronomically in cost. Inflation had hit Israel hard, a tiny country burdened with the world's highest tax rate and an army and reserve that included everyone out of a wheelchair. Schoenbaum wanted not only a house, but a piece of property, a foothold on history. In America he was content in an apartment; in Israel he wanted the Promised Land.

Finally, on a stony hillside near the northern edge of the city limits, so far away from civilization you could hardly hear the rock band at the Tel Aviv Hilton, Schoenbaum grabbed Harold's shoulder, almost causing him to swerve off the road.

"Stop the car!" he shouted. "This could be the place!" Harold jammed on the brakes, and Schoenbaum was out of the car before it stopped rolling. The others followed, trying to see what had caused all the excitement.

The old man turned to Uncle Zvi.

"You got a listing on this house?" he inquired. "How much down, bottom line? Remember this is Schoenbaum."

"A house? What house? A shack I see, a broken building, no roof, but a house, no."

"To you it's a shack. To me, Schoenbaum, it's a palace. I'm a carpenter, I'll build; I'm an electrician, I'll wire; I'm a contractor, I'll fight City Hall!"

"Papa!" reminded Sonya. "You're seventy-five years old!"

"Sixty," said her father. "Remember, you're nineteen."

"I wouldn't sell this dump to my worst enemy," protested Uncle Zvi.

All Schoenbaum needed to make up his mind was a little opposition. "How much do you want for it?"

"Three times what it's worth."

"I can't afford a penny more than twice. Take it or leave it."

"I think you got a deal, partner," said Uncle Zvi unhappily. He liked Schoenbaum, who he had discovered was a fellow pinochle addict. He took off his ten-gallon hat and got his notebook out of it. Chaim-Harold had always felt he carried a telephone in there, too, but he hadn't been able to prove it.

"When can I move in?"

"I would suggest tomorrow," said Uncle Zvi. "In the morning, before it falls down."

On the ride home Schoenbaum sat in the back with Zvi to conclude the details. Sonya sat up front with Harold, holding his free hand, mainly in self-defense. She was unhappy about her father's decision; it would take months to put the old house in shape. It was far away from the bright lights of Dizengoff Street, and it was in an area strewn with craggy rocks, of volcanic origin, Harold informed her between gropings. By the way, would it be possible for him to visit her in her room later that night, after the old man had truly gone to sleep?

"Shhhh," whispered Sonya, "I don't know. We'd have to be absolutely silent."

"That's the way I like it. Afterward we could write notes."

He smiled at her again. She was beginning to like his smile. But he was presuming too much.

"I didn't exactly say yes," whispered Sonya.

"You didn't exactly say no," Chaim-Harold reminded her. And smiled again.

At that precise moment Israel's Prime Minister was receiving an unexpected visit from his chief of intelligence. The Prime Minister, who had come into office during what had become known as the Jewish Watergate, following Yitzhak Rabin's resignation, had been getting ready for bed and was in his robe. He greeted the chief as if this were a nightly occurrence, which it was.

"Shimon," he admonished for the hundredth time, "you could have called on the hot line; that's supposed to be used for crises."

"It's always busy," Shimon Gan reminded him with a sigh. He extended a large photograph. "You had to see this for yourself. Our neighbors don't know the Americans are supplying us with these satellite pictures. Incidentally, neither do the Americans."

His host knew it was true. Photographs from the eye-in-the-sky spy satellites are beamed to earth on secret radio frequencies, scrambled in transmission, and have to be unscrambled at earth stations, like coded messages. Only recently had Israeli intelligence succeeded in unscrambling the pictures for themselves. It gave them a feeling of security, like having a closed-circuit camera in your girlfriend's bedroom.

The Prime Minister examined the photographs with a soldier's eye. Taken with 1000mm lenses on heat-sensitive film, they indicated with bright dots the location of any sizable engines, camouflaged or not. Several areas near Israel's northern flank and in the Sinai showed an unusually large number of dots. Undoubtedly tanks, he concluded.

"Exactly," said his intelligence chief. "Our friends have quite a problem. Everyone is selling or giving them tanks; the price is so good and they've acquired so many they obviously have no place to keep them, so they're moving them to our borders. Pretty soon, they may decide there isn't any place to keep them except *inside* our borders.''

"A universal problem." The Prime Minister nodded. "No parking space. I feel for them."

"What's our next move? Build them a garage?"

"I don't think so. Obviously, Plan B is being activated. I think we should appeal to the United Nations. We could use a good laugh."

He looked thoughtfully out of the window toward the south, where God and Moses and Cecil B. De Mille had parted the Red Sea.

"Or," he said quietly, "a good miracle."

If God heard him, He gave no sign.

At that moment.

Sonya waited in her room at the Waldorf-Astoria, in her robe, until it was well past midnight. She knew it was wrong, she hardly knew the boy, this was no way to start making a name for herself in a strange country, but there was no denying the attraction she felt for Chaim-Harold. Convention was unimportant. If she were truly liberated, nothing mattered but her emotions. There would be time enough to think it over later. This is what she had been taught by her peers at Sarah Lawrence; Sonya wanted to live up to their image.

There was a knock, and she felt her heart pounding. She arranged the robe provocatively and opened the door.

"Shame on you," said Schoenbaum, pushing his way in. "Close up the bathrobe, sit down on the bed, we'll talk; nobody should say is by Schoenbaum a daughter a pushover."

Never had he spoken to her this way; she had always been his little angel.

"Papa, I don't know what you mean."

"I promised your mother, may she rest in peace. Until

tonight, I didn't believe her. Sonya, it's in the Bible, 'Thou shalt not commit adultery.' ''

"You can't commit adultery unless you're married. There's nothing in the Ten Commandments about not doing it when you're *not* married."

"God didn't think it would come up, with a Nice Jewish Girl. God can't know everything. Who is He, Walter Cronkite?''

In spite of herself, Sonya felt her heart going out to him. My God, she thought, seventy-five years old, and for the first time he's going to try to tell me about the birds and the bees.

"Papa," she said, "I like this boy very much, I don't know if anything might happen tonight, but I have the right to make my own mistakes, haven't I?"

"I want to tell you something," Schoenbaum said slowly. "When I married your mother, she hadn't ever done it. I hadn't ever done it. Nobody even told us how you did it. Our old rabbi, he wasn't married, he hadn't ever done it, although he showed us some pretty hotsy-totsy sections in the Bible. Grapes, melons, who could figure out? So our honeymoon was beautiful. For a whole day Sophie locked herself in the bathroom; the waiter passed in the food through the window. When she finally came out, sweet, loving, because Schoenbaum had waited, we still didn't know how. So it was Columbus discovering America. After a while, aha! Land ho! Believe me, never in my life has there been again something this beautiful. But with you, what's beautiful? Every day Columbus Day!''

"Papa, listen," Sonya said, "it's different now. A girl is supposed to enjoy. Whatever you want is good for you."

"For forty-three years I slept with your mother. What I wanted was Greta Garbo. Did it kill me?''

"Were you happy?"

"What's happy got to do? We were *married*."

"That's not important."

"Why? Happy is all that counts? Shtupping is why God

went to all the trouble, worked six days? Who works six days anymore? Why do you think your mother told me to bring you? In New York everybody was talking. Here, in the Holy Land, maybe you would be our Sonya again. I'm an old man. I would like maybe to have a grandson, is it so terrible? But I don't want to be a grandfather only because my daughter forgot a pill. It's not the same, not for you, not for me, not for the baby. Not for your mother, may she rest. I want a son-in-law to holler on, I want a grandson should get chocolate on me; when I call him a little bastard, it should be *my* idea, not yours. Sonya, this is Israel. In this country every Jew can hold his head up. Why should your father be the only one who can't?''

And then, realizing he had said too much, he stood up abruptly and became Schoenbaum again.

"Go, do what you want!" he hollered. "Hang out a sign, Sonya the Nafka, Wholesale and Retail, I should worry. You killed your mother, so kill your father, but first of all, enjoy. In Macy's window." He turned away, so she shouldn't see Schoenbaum upset.

Sonya got to her feet, deeply touched. The man who could defeat City Hall was surrendering to his daughter. Napoleon was retreating from Moscow. She didn't want to see it. She crossed and took his hand.

"Papa, I'll try," she said. "I'll try to be an old-fashioned girl at this late date. At least, I'll be a novelty."

She kissed him then, the first time since she was a little girl, just as there came an impatient knock at the door. Sonya threw it open, revealing Chaim-Harold, carrying a bottle of Carmel wine and an extremely hopeful expression.

"Come in, come in," she cried, "and let Papa horsewhip you."

5 Schoenbaum Strikes Seltzer

Kikar Malchei, in Hebrew, means Square of the Kings. It is here in Tel Aviv that the municipal buildings stand, a little less regal than the name of the square might imply, inhabited by officials whose authority is somewhat less than that of King Solomon, although none of them will admit it. Since the mayor of Tel Aviv must deal continuously with a constituency so hardened by adversity they make New York City's irate taxpayers seem pantywaists, even Jacob Schoenbaum found it impossible to break through the cordon of security around Kikar Malchei and surrounding the mayor. He found himself shunted into the tiny office of the assistant water commissioner. It didn't improve Schoenbaum's disposition, never noted for its calm reasonableness.

"What kind nonsense you call this?" he asked, outraged, waving his water bill above his head.

The assistant commissioner, a calm, middle-aged official toughened by years of adversary action against a citizenry which had survived more than one holocaust and was singularly uncowed by authority, looked up wearily. "Pay the bill or get out," he said in what for him was a kindly manner.

"I'm in my house one week, I get a bill for six months! The roof isn't even on yet, you're charging a fortune for water tastes like it's from Yasir Arafat's mikvah. I want you to know, I'm not paying!"

Schoenbaum was used to anything but indifference. It was unnerving. The commissioner merely shrugged. He, too, didn't know the mettle of the old man with whom he was dealing. The irresistible force was meeting the immovable object.

"Fine," said the commissioner. "Don't pay the bill, we'll cut off the water. You want to be a shlimazl, be a shlimazl. Now get out."

"This is how you talk to a guest from America?"

"This is Israel. It's also how we talk to the Prime Minister."

Recognizing this undeniable truth, Schoenbaum shifted his attack. "You've tasted the water?" he inquired angrily.

"What am I, crazy? I drink Schweppes Bitter Lemon."

"You're the assistant commissioner, you should taste!"

"The power commissioner sticks his fingers in electric sockets? Pay the bill. Leave me alone."

"Don't speak this way to an old man!"

"I'm older than you are."

"You don't look it."

"I know, I don't drink the water. Now get out, shlimazl. I'm busy."

Schoenbaum leaned over his desk. "Nobody plays games with Schoenbaum!" he warned. "I'll dig a well, put you out of business!"

The commissioner started to laugh. He hadn't had a good laugh in a month, what with his official duties and his wife's cooking.

"So, dig!" he said. "You know how far down you have to

go in Israel to find water? Why do you think we can charge so much? Go ahead, try, you could dig until the Second Coming, which I personally don't intend to wait for." He laughed again; it might be his last in a long time—his wife had threatened Fondue Bourgignone that night. The laugh became a chortle.

That did it. The old man's inviolate pride had been attacked. He drew himself up to his full five feet four. At this moment he seemed much taller. Five feet five possibly.

"I'll dig," declared Jacob Schoenbaum. "I'll dig, maybe to China. I won't stop until I find. But I guarantee I'll find. Remember, Schoenbaum said it." And he was gone, swiftly. Another good exit.

The assistant commissioner sat up, worriedly, in his swivel chair. There had been a conviction in the old man's voice that rang a bell. Somewhere in the deep recesses of his mind, he had heard that voice before. Joan of Arc, calling to the people of France. Abraham, calling the Israelites together in the Wilderness. The Lord, addressing Moses, as he handed him the Eleventh Commandment, and Moses immediately got rid of his secretary.

Chaim-Harold Bernstein was not a man to mark time, especially where his love life was involved. He had been a frequent visitor to the Schoenbaum establishment, bringing little gifts calculated to put him on target—Sonya. There were confiscated cigars for her father, confiscated perfume for Sonya, all the little perquisites a job in the Customs Service provides its faithful employees. There had been one drawback, however. Through the window of the unfinished living room he would see the determined old man dragging a huge beam to help support the roof or wheeling a load of cement to the back patio. Harold would feel obliged to get up from the sofa, where he and Sonya were engaged in intimate conversation, and lend his young strength to the operation. The problem was that Harold's young strength included a weak back; he was too proud to mention it, but after an hour of lifting, hauling, and pushing, he was in no shape to pursue his romantic intentions with Sonya. Thus, when she told him her father would be spending the entire day in Tel Aviv to holler about the water, Harold leaped at the opportunity to be alone with his lady love without running the danger of a double hernia.

By this time Sonya and Harold had, surprisingly, developed an honest affection for each other. She found Harold something of a poet, a dreamer, and an idealist, albeit with an overdeveloped sex drive. Possibly, when she found time, she would make him a character in her first novel, which was coming along well, as she had just purchased some typing paper and was thinking about buying a typewriter. Harold had sacrificed a great deal in his chosen field to come to this little country. Perhaps it is the aura of history, in the dim past and the dangerous present, that attracts the young of many nations to the life in Israel, with its constant turmoil, its indigestible felafel, and its impossible economy. More possibly, it is the sense of purpose, the pioneering fight for survival, that appeals to a younger generation in search of belonging. In large nations you seldom get to know your next-door neighbor. In Israel the entire population is a moving target, and it makes for a certain camaraderie. For Harold, this was reason enough for being here; perhaps later his particular talents could be better employed. For now he would gripe along with the sabras about the climate, the food, the danger, but he secretly gave thanks for the Arabs. They were his City Hall; like Schoenbaum, the fight kept him young. He had been growing soft and purposeless, and he didn't like the soft, purposeless young ladies of his set in Dallas. In Sonya he felt a kindred pioneering spirit. As he held her in his arms on the couch in the almost-finished living room, he tried a little pioneering of his own. Sonya pulled away.

"No," she said, "Harold, I can't."

"You got a bad back, too?"

"No. But I promised Papa, until I'm married, I'll do nothing."

"Fine. I didn't promise anybody; you just lie there doing nothing, leave the rest to me."

She sat up. "Harold, listen to me," she said. "After we're married, we can have each other for forty-three years. Why rush?"

"Would it be so terrible if it was forty-two and a half and we started now?"

"Yes," Sonya told him, "it would cheapen both of us."

"Sonya, I'm not going to promise to do something for forty-three years before I know if I like it for ten minutes. Maybe fifteen."

"You're going to make me do something terrible before even marrying me?"

"If it's so terrible, why do you want to keep doing it for forty-three years?"

"I don't!" shouted Sonya, her father's daughter at last. "I hate you, Chaim Barak! I also hate you, Harold Bernstein! Get out, both of you!"

Harold's answer was to grab her and kiss her. For a moment she struggled, resisting. Gradually, she stopped fighting and started helping.

And then the earth moved.

It startled both of them. For an instant they separated. And then Harold took Sonya in his arms and kissed her once more, fiercely.

The earth moved again.

Tears filled Sonya's eyes. Ernest Hemingway had been right. She and Harold were fated for each other.

How could they know that in the Negev Desert near the atomic reactor at Dimona, Israel had detonated its first secret underground explosion? Nobody knew. Nobody was to know for a long time, and then few believed. All Sonya and Harold understood was that they had kissed each other in anger and the earth had moved for them. Perhaps they had better not kiss again until Schoenbaum finished shoring up the roof.

When the old man returned from the assistant water commissioner's office, his blood pressure at a new high, the happy couple met him at the doorway.

"Papa," Sonya announced, starry-eyed, "Harold and I are going to get married!"

"Why?"

Knowing Sonya, it was a fair question.

"The earth moved," she said, simply.

"Oy!" said her father. "The cesspool I dug, it's caving in."

"No cesspool," said Harold. "True love."

And he kissed Sonya so that Schoenbaum could see the truth with his own eyes.

It was an emotional moment. The promise the old man had given Sophie was about to be fulfilled. The impossible dream had materialized. Schoenbaum wanted to say something to these two wonderful children, to show the depths of his feeling, but for a moment he couldn't speak. Finally, the words came to him.

"I got some slivovitz," said Schoenbalum, "could blow off the top of your head."

From a locked cabinet he took a precious bottle. Slivovitz is made from fermented prune pits and, it is rumored, plutonium.

Schoenbaum poured a large drink into each of three water glasses and handed Sonya and Harold theirs. One could almost see the steam rise.

"L'chayim," he said, raising his glass in the traditional toast to life, and tossed it down, neat. Harold, who had gotten a quick whiff of his own drink, expected to see smoke rising from the old man's eyes, but they merely watered a bit.

Schoenbaum looked at him, accusingly. "You're not drinking L'chayim?"

The implication was that Harold's intentions were not truly honorable.

Sonya took Harold's glass and her own and crossed to the sink in the kitchen.

"Papa," she called, "if we drank your slivovitz straight, we'd have a funeral, not a wedding." And she held a glass under the faucet and turned on the tap. There was a gurgling sound, and the slivovitz started to disappear upward into the pipes.

"That shlemiel in the Kikar Malchei!" shouted Schoenbaum, instantly apoplectic. "He's turned off the water! He won't get away with it! We'll start digging the well!"

"Wouldn't it be easier to pay the bill?" Sonya suggested.

"And give him the satisfaction? Never! I'll die first!" He turned to Harold. "From college you got a degree how to dig; in the morning we'll begin, first thing!"

Harold felt twinges in his back from the mere thought. "Nobody knows how far down the water table is here," he protested.

"Moses brought water from a stone; it's in the Bible, happened down the street someplace. We might only have to go down a couple feet; that shlemiel in the Kikar Malchei will get heartburn!"

"But, Papa, what about our wedding?" Fear was clutching at Sonya. She knew her father's obsession with City Hall. How long could she keep Harold in the mood without breaking her sacred, old-fashioned promise?

"Without water, how can we have a wedding? I promised your mother, not a synagogue, the wedding in the house, it's nicer."

"We could get married in City Hall," said Harold foolishly.

"Over my dead body!" shouted Schoenbaum. "In this house the ceremony; we'll invite friends, pinochle players, everybody. Also, why spend money for a hotel, the honeymoon you can have right here; and who can have a honeymoon, no water?''

"Maybe we could use a Wash 'n' Dry," suggested Harold, impatiently. He wanted the argument to be over so the forty-three years of enjoyment could begin. Sonya took his hand consolingly.

Schoenbaum looked at the lovers and remembered how it had been. "All right," he said, softly—for Schoenbaum. "You won't have to wait long, there's a big company in Tel Aviv, Sahara Jiffy Well Drillers, I'll pay them to start in the morning; by night we'll hit water, we'll send out the invitations."

Like many good ideas, this one didn't work out as planned. The Sahara Jiffy Well Drillers arrived and set up their massive equipment. An impatient Harold Bernstein surveyed the geological probabilities of Schoenbaum's hillside and selected a site where there was a slight fissure in the solid rock. With luck, he felt, the drill would reach the water table before he died of lack of enjoyment.

Night and day the Jiffy Well Drillers worked, Schoenbaum driving them on. Night and day the engine clattered away, keeping the distant neighbors awake as it ground through the rock with a sound like a thousand dentists at work on a Medicare patient. They struck granite, but never water. The cost of fighting City Hall rose to astronomical heights as the well sank lower.

"For two hundred Israeli pounds," a frantic daughter reminded Schoenbaum, "the city will be glad to turn the water back on!" Grimly, her father refused. Millions for defense, not one agora for that shlemiel in the Kikar Malchei. The Jiffy Well Drillers announced the jiffy was over, they were admitting defeat and abandoning the job. Schoenbaum paid them to leave their machinery in place, and after they left, he kept the drill running single-handedly. When the shaft reached a depth of eight hundred and fifty feet, Schoenbaum felt a twinge of his old rheumatism returning. It could mean only one thing: The well was approaching water. But he was too tired to go any further that night. Wearily, he turned off the engine, stopped the clatter of the drill, and dragged himself to the couch in the living room.

He was asleep before his tired body hit the cushions, so he had no way of seeing Chaim-Harold crawl in through the window behind him, take off his shoes, and sneak up the stairs to the bedroom, where the somewhat virginal Sonya was awaiting him.

This was the night they both had decided it was foolish to delay the inevitable. After all, Sonya wouldn't be nineteen forever, maybe just five or six more years.

She received her lover with open arms, and in a few moments they were in the marriage bed, slightly in advance of the ceremony, but Sonya felt the Lord would be understanding, especially if He knew Schoenbaum.

The earth moved again.

This time, however, they were too occupied to notice.

There were loud rumblings from deep below the rock strata, the house actually shook, but Jacob Schoenbaum, on his couch, remained sleeping. He did not feel the sudden twinge in his left knee that should have warned him.

Noah, awaken, God is singing "Anchors Aweigh"!

A climax was approaching, upstairs and down. The plumbing, which Schoenbaum had connected to the wellhead in hopeful anticipation, suddenly trembled in the walls of the old building. Upstairs, where the premature honeymoon was in progress, Sonya's bathroom, where all the valves had been left open to reduce pressure, turned, appropriately, into Niagara Falls. Like most rooms in Israel, Sonya's bedroom was tiny; the bathroom door was open; the sudden force of the shower drenched the bed completely, although it must be said in Harold's defense he didn't become waterlogged for a full thirty seconds, which speaks well for his powers of concentration. Only then, as he sat up and received a mouthful of water from Schoenbaum's Well, did the full significance of the moment hit him. He raced out of the bedroom and down the stairs, shouting for Schoenbaum, forgetful of the fact that he was better dressed for the Garden of Eden than for Pinsker Street, Tel Aviv.

The old man struggled awake on the couch to find his daughter's intended charging down the stairway from her room, stark naked, and hollering on Schoenbaum. At the same time water was erupting from the kitchen sink, bubbling and sizzling.

"The water!" Harold was hollering. "It's not just water!" From its brackish nature, its color, and its taste, he knew it was from the pool that collects on the surface of an oil deposit.

"Oil!" he shouted. "You've struck oil!"

"You momzer, where are your pants?" Schoenbaum shouted back, still trying to clear his mind of sleep. "What are you doing here, it's midnight?"

"The fissure! The fissure!" shouted Harold incoherently. "She opened up wide!"

"Her name is Schoenbaum, not Fisher!" shouted the old man angrily. "You shouldn't talk about a nice girl this way."

"No! No! The well! It's coming in!"

Schoenbaum, still not fully awake, chose this moment to reach for his security blanket, his Manuelo y Vega.

"Don't light it!" cried Harold, making a grab for it, but he was too late. Schoenbaum had already struck a match.

There was a considerable amount of natural gas coming through the plumbing along with the brackish water. Schoenbaum had noticed the bubbling while he was lighting the match but hadn't been too alarmed; it seemed only natural that in Israel a person could strike seltzer.

There was a sudden flash and a roar that eventually was to be heard around the world. The north side of Schoenbaum's renovated home blew into the street, along with Schoenbaum, Chaim-Harold, and Sonya herself. They landed in the huge pile of powdered stone excavated from the well and were not harmed, except emotionally, since two of them were stark naked.

From Schoenbaum's Well, a geyser was appearing, black, sticky, smearing the air. It caught the flame from the fire, and its burning glow appeared like a moving finger in the night sky, spelling out a message for all the Arab world to see:

MENE, MENE, TEKEL, UPHARSIN.

6 Hot Mama
Burns Her Strudel

MIDNIGHT IN Tel Aviv is three o'clock in the afternoon at the United Nations Building in New York. The General Assembly was meeting to consider a resolution presented by the foreign minister of Abu Dhabi. Only a few years earlier, if you had asked the average New Yorker what Abu Dhabi was, he probably would have replied it was the opening line of "Aba Daba Honeymoon," sung by Rudy Vallee in 1928—that is, if he bothered to answer you at all. Had you told him it was a trucial sheikhdom on the Persian Gulf whose oil reserves made those of the state of Texas resemble a small jar of Vaseline, he might well have called a cop. But today Abu Dhabi is a respected member of the Organization of Petroleum Exporting Countries. Its oil wealth is so tremendous and its population so small that it has been said that every Abu Dhabian gets Blue Cross and an American Express card at birth. It has been rumored that a recent ruling of the Abu Dhabian courts declared the houris of Sheikh Nabayon's harem to have been unlawfully indentured, and they were made free agents.

The bidding among wealthy Abu Dhabians for their services became so spirited one talented courtesan with a record of fourteen wins and no defeats in a single evening brought the equivalent of the price of two Catfish Hunters. When she and three other equally athletic ladies were acquired by the same wealthy sheikh, the purchase was greeted with angry cries of "Break up the Yankees!"

The story may be apocryphal, but there is nothing apocryphal about Abu Dhabi itself, the most affluent per square inch of all the OPEC nations. Consequently, Abu Dhabi was chosen to launch the penultimate stage of Plan B. This was in the form of a United Nations resolution calling on Israel to give back not only the territory it had captured from the Arab world, but also all the rest of its territory except for a narrow strip along the Dead Sea that has neither drinking water nor vegetation. What it has a lot of is salt; it was figured that this, plus a little chicken fat, would suffice to support the population. The Israeli army, navy, and air force were to be turned over to the Palestine Liberation Organization as a gesture of goodwill. After this was done, the Geneva peace conference would finally be convened, the security of Israel now assured. Even if the Arab world managed to push the Jewish population into the sea, in the Dead Sea they would float. It was a humanitarian solution.

The United States delegation went into immediate caucus. The U.S. ambassador felt so strongly about the incredible callousness of the Abu Dhabian resolution that he saw no other course for his great nation but to defy the implicit threat of another Arab oil embargo and act in the historical tradition of liberty and justice of the United States of America by abstaining. Cooler heads prevailed, however, and he finally was persuaded to call in sick.

The final vote was an overwhelming 110 to 0 in favor of the Abu Dhabian resolution against Israel, with 14 abstentions, 11 calling in sick, and 9 stuck in traffic, out of gas.

Plan B was on schedule.

It is not generally known, but Rov Aluf Shemuhl Kishner was the brains behind the Entebbe raid, now celebrated in song, story, and television. A dedicated soldier, vice-chief of the Israeli army's Intelligence Service, Kishner served under Shimon Gan. It was said of him, only half in jest, that he had the kind of vision Moshe Dayan might have had if he took off that eye patch. The greatest mystery of Entebbe is where Prime Minister Idi Amin Dada was spending the night while the raid was taking place. Kishner held the key. During the Ugandan dictator's period of training as a paratrooper with the Israeli air force it had been Kishner's official assignment to provide him with feminine companionship, to put it in its most polite, or congressional, terms. Kishner had gone about it methodically, as he did everything else. He issued precise orders to several lady soldiers, who promptly refused, claiming the new army regulations precluded their participation in armed combat. Several of them claimed, in addition, to have weak backs and, like Chaim-Harold, to be incapable of lifting heavy loads. Forced to seek civilian aid, Kishner located Nadya Haffaz, Israel's fattest belly dancer, whose measurements were 46-54-who counts?

Nadya and the mountainous Amin hit it off immediately; her belly dance training stood her in good stead. Amin was so intrigued with her muscular control he arranged with Kishner to have her visit him at the secret paratroop field in the Negev every weekend. Nadya herself was overjoyed at finding a dancing partner who approached her own dimensions. Inducted into the army, she threw herself into her assignment with such dedication she made corporal in only two weekends. When the dictator left to return to his own country, a tearful Nadya gave him a keepsake: one of her favorite G-strings, three and a half lovely yards of sparkling rhinestones, still warm.

So the logistics of the Entebbe raid were simple: three C-30s, one hundred trained commandos, two armored cars, two jeeps, the famous black Mercedes, and a parachute large enough for Nadya. She had been keeping telephone contact with her amour and had, at the behest of Shimon Gan, arranged a rendezvous with him for the night of the raid. Since there was no way for her to cross the border unseen, she had suggested to him that she be parachuted into his mountain hideaway. Amin had been intrigued by the adventurous aspect of such an undertaking. Also, the sight of Nadya descending from an altitude of five thousand feet in her G-string was something calculated to stir the pulse of the most jaded prime minister. Disraeli himself might have felt his juices flow at such a view of so much Nice Jewish Girl.

Nadya landed with a slight thud in a clearing near Amin's mountain hideaway and managed somehow to keep him interested for the twelve hours before the raid was scheduled to begin. After that, she kept him *very* interested. It is a matter of record that when his chief of staff attempted to telephone the prime minister from the Entebbe Airport while the attack was in progress, the phone rang twelve times before Amin could get a hand free to answer it. Even then he didn't seem pleased about being interrupted. "Remember what I told you when you applied for the job?" he shouted. "Don't call me, I'll call you!" He turned back to Nadya, and the rest is history.

Shemuhl Kishner had no time to take bows for his achievement. His duties kept him too busy for such trifles as decorations or promotions. The months passed by, and every night, almost routinely, he was awakened from his sleep to cope with an emergency, since the fedayeen always attacked under cover of darkness. This midnight started out no differently from many others. A routine assignment: a bomb presumably exploded near Pinsker Street, a house on fire. Fatalities unknown. Enemy unseen. In eighty-four seconds Kishner had his pants on, his uniform buttoned, and was heading for the jeep always at the ready in the driveway of intelligence headquarters, where he slept. He was a man who had no patience for any but the Spartan attributes of life. The rumor had it that on the few occasions Kishner had a woman to his room, he would set an egg timer. Medium-boiled was all his schedule allowed.

Tonight everything was going according to plan. His driver was already in the jeep; an armored personnel carrier was moving out of the driveway with the search squad; the glow of the fire was visible on the hill only a few miles away, in the suburbs beyond the Tel Aviv Hilton. The jeep shot away toward the hill. By Kishner's reckoning, in one hour the PLO would issue a bulletin claiming responsibility for the bomb, within twenty-four hours the United Nations would again order Israel to give back all captured territory, and within forty-eight hours another bomb would go off. You could set your egg timer by it.

As he arrived on the scene of Schoenbaum's Well, he noted something strangely different. The fire was burning far beyond the limits of the usual plastic explosive; flames were shooting ninety and one hundred feet into the air, accompanied by a roaring sound. The crowd was huge, attracted from pinochle games, the Omar Khayyam nightclub, and bed by the magnitude of the explosion. An old man was hollering on the fire department that it was all the fault of some shlemiel in the Kikar Malchei. Temporary ropes had been strung up to hold back the crowd from the danger area, two fire department trucks were spraying water on the fire and the old man, without much visible result, and as Kishner leaped from the jeep, he saw a furtive figure in an Arab caftan leaving the scene. Kishner was on him in an instant, a well-practiced flying tackle throwing the fugitive to the ground.

"For Christ sake," cried Chaim-Harold, "get everybody away, there's going to be another explosion!"

Kishner had his gun to Harold's head. "Put up your hands or I'll blow your brains out," he said routinely.

"If I put up my hands," Harold protested, "my sheet will fall off."

It was true; Sonya had found the sheet among the debris and draped it about her lover, not dreaming it would cause him to be mistaken for one of the hated fedayeen. Kishner cocked his pistol, the sheet fell off, and the vice-chief of intelligence, a keen observer, took one look and loosened his grip on the trigger.

"You're Jewish!" he informed Harold, to whom it wasn't exactly news. "Pull up the sheet and tell me what you're doing, throwing bombs?"

Harold draped the sheet about himself quickly and tried to make Kishner understand. This wasn't a bomb; a water well was being drilled. Somehow, in a way that even Harold didn't understand yet, at a depth of only eight hundred fifty feet a major oil deposit that hadn't existed only a week ago, when Harold made his survey for water, had suddenly been tapped. The force of the hidden gas and oil was so great it was geysering up out of the ground. Schoenbaum's cigar had ignited the gas, and the fire department was only spreading the oil and inviting catastrophe by pouring water on it. Something had to be done!

Only one word of what Harold was telling him registered on Kishner's trained senses: oil. His eyes, his nose, all his acute senses told him there might be truth in it. His mind told him, if it's true, nobody must know, a theory that has guided the intelligence services of the world since time immemorial. In a flash he was at the radio in his jeep, gripping the microphone tensely, pressing the press-to-talk switch that would put him into instant communication with intelligence headquarters. It must be pointed out that, in the interests of economy, the Israeli army has installed sophisticated Citizen Band units from the United States for mobile communications in nonsensitive areas. The frequencies are specifically reserved for the military.

"446, this is 022," Kishner whispered into the microphone. "Code 999," he added, using the secret cipher for extreme urgency.

"Hello, good buddy," responded a warm female voice.

"This is Hot Mama over by Ben Yehuda Street. Don't floor it, just spotted Smokey heading west near Yeshiva University."

Kishner cursed the enterprising Tel Aviv radio dealer who had imported a thousand cheap CB sets from the U.S., even though their public use was illegal in Israel.

"Get off the channel!" Kishner whispered into the mike. "I order you off the air! This is Rov Aluf Kishner on secret assignment!"

"Shemuhl! This is Aunt Becky! You want I should run down by intelligence and tell them they should turn on the radio?"

"Aunt Becky? You're Hot Mama?"

"Except to your uncle. By nine o'clock he's asleep, Raquel Welch couldn't keep him up. I even tried making strudel, didn't help."

"022, this is 446," broke in a crisp voice. "Were you attempting contact?"

Kishner breathed a sigh of relief. Headquarters at last.

"Yes. Code 999."

"Listen, Headquarters," Aunt Becky reported, "there's a big fire up by Schoenbaum's, the meshuggener. Hurry. Code 999 means 'emergency.'"

"Aunt Becky, get off the radio!"

"I'm only trying to help, maybe he doesn't have his secret code book, I got mine only yesterday by the radio store, they were out."

"He's got one, he's got one! Headquarters, Code 999, immediate reinforcements, top priority, inform Bluebird."

"Bluebird is the Prime Minister, in case you didn't get the book, Headquarters."

"Aunt Becky, get off the air, goddammit!" shouted her nephew, whose rank of rov aluf is equivalent to lieutenant general. Sometimes.

"Listen, Shemuhl, what's going on by Schoenbaum's? It smells like kerosene is burning."

Kishner almost dropped the microphone. He knew the frequencies they were using were under constant surveillance by Syrian monitoring stations. Aunt Becky's lucky guess could be reported to Premier Affaz within five minutes. He turned to the armored personnel carrier and ordered it to 56 Ben Yehuda Street to neutralize Aunt Becky.

Fortunately, she had enough strudel to go around.

7 The Pinsker Street Gusher Blows In

THE ISRAELI CABINET was accustomed to being summoned to emergency meetings, usually to hear a visiting American secretary of state explain that permanent peace had finally been agreed on with the Arab League and the Palestine Liberation Organization. There had been at least three permanent peaces in the last few years, two of them accompanied by attacks across the Suez Canal. The ministers could be excused for a feeling of *déjà vu* when they were summoned once more by the prime minister, this time to the penthouse meeting room of the Tel Aviv Hilton, close to the scene of *L'Affaire* Schoenbaum.

By this hour the army had succeeded in blowing out the oil fire at the Schoenbaum Well through the use of explosives, and a cover story about a fedayeen bomb attempt on the lives of Schoenbaum, Sonya, and Harold had been distributed to the press. Schoenbaum, eagerly going along with the deception, had wanted to have the bombing attributed to Mayor Abraham

Beame, but it was pointed out to him that unfortunately, Beame was Jewish, and the allegation might be counterproductive.

It was a moment that would be recorded in history books, at least those not destroyed by the Israeli government in the later cover-up attempt, when the Prime Minister strode into the conference room to face his Cabinet with his chief of staff, Schoenbaum, Chaim-Harold, Rov Aluf Kishner, and Aluf Mordechai Haimowitz, chief of the Israeli Defense Forces' Geological Survey Unit.

Israel's Chief of State called the meeting to order. He was a no-nonsense leader, a man of and for the people. His face betrayed little emotion, but there was a feeling of exultation in the air, exultation tempered with bitter experience. Every time something good had happened to the little nation, John Foster Dulles or Henry Kissinger had snatched it away. This time the secret must be kept until it was too late for their great friend Uncle Sam to louse it up.

"Gentlemen," he said, "a discovery has been made in our little country that, if it is of the magnitude we believe it to be, can well change the future of our nation. One of our new immigrants, a courageous, forceful, determined, and patriotic hero—"

"I'm still not paying the water bill!" Schoenbaum shouted. He was not one to be easily soft-soaped by City Hall.

The Chief of State attempted to smile. As Prime Minister he was well aware of the nature of his constituency. It was composed of three million Schoenbaums. Sometimes he had difficulty forcing himself out of bed in the morning.

"We'll get to the water bill later," he said.

"*Now,*" insisted Schoenbaum. "Turn on the water so Sonya can have a wedding at the house, like I promised her mother, God should rest her soul. A girl has a right to enjoy; she shouldn't have to wait."

"It will be taken care of. You have my word of honor as Prime Minister."

"In this country tomorrow you could be running a candy

store. I would like now to have it in black and white, on a piece paper.''

Schoenbaum's opponent hesitated. It was insane to be standing here, the Prime Minister of a sovereign nation, arguing with a little old man about his water bill in front of the entire Cabinet. But he controlled himself; secrecy was of the utmost importance at this point, and Schoenbaum was the legal owner of the property on which the oil had been found. Without his silence and cooperation, things could get sticky.

The Chief of State of the nation of Israel turned to his minister of the interior. ''Turn on the water for our friend Schoenbaum,'' he said. ''Immediately.''

''It will be done,'' the minister assured him.

''Immediately means today, not tomorrow,'' Schoenbaum reminded him.

The minister of the interior controlled himself after a frantic signal from his Chief. ''You have my word,'' he said finally.

''I would prefer in black and white, on a piece paper.''

The minister muttered a few choice words in Hebrew, a language that has served both the Lord and Solomon's wives adequately in moments of stress. Fortunately, no one heard. The minister pulled out his ball-point pen and wrote an order for Schoenbaum's water to be turned back on.

He wrote it in black and white, on a piece paper.

Schoenbaum subsided, City Hall having gone into full retreat, and returned his attention to the Prime Minister's announcement.

''Last night, on the property of our patriotic friend Schoenbaum, a drill he was using to probe for water broke through the rock into something that caused a tremendous release of underground pressure and, eventually, an explosion and fire.''

''I was smoking at the time a cigar, Manuelo y Vega,'' Schoenbaum interjected, ''Havana. Give credit where credit is due.''

Israel's leader smiled the same tense smile. He seemed to twitch a little.

"He was smoking at the time a cigar, Manuelo y Vega," said the Premier, "Havana."

"Cuba," added Schoenbaum, a stickler for accuracy.

"Cuba," repeated the Prime Minister, still smiling. "As you know, our nation has some oil wells in the vicinity of Ashdod, and there is also offshore oil in the Gulf of Suez presently in dispute with the government of Egypt. But these are minor deposits, difficult to exploit. The Schoenbaum Well is an anomaly, in an area thought to be nonproductive, in the very heart of our country, on Minsker Street, Tel Aviv—"

"*Pinsker* Street," corrected Schoenbaum. "How come when you send me a water bill you get the address right?"

"*Pinsker* Street," said the Premier, twitching again. "Shortly after it erupted, our alert Intelligence Service arrived on the scene. Rov Aluf Kishner, whose services to the nation you are familiar with—" he indicated Kishner, who acknowledged, with a slight nod of his head, the ripple of applause from several Cabinet ministers who had also been introduced to Nadya Haffaz.

"Rov Aluf Kishner," continued the prime minister, "will tell you what he found after the explosion."

Kishner stood, slowly, and pulled from a pocket a neat pad, on which he had made his meticulous notes.

"Twelve thirteen," he read. "Arrived at fire to detain suspicious Arab fleeing scene. Claimed to be Chaim Barak, born Harold Bernstein, Dallas, Texas, U.S.A. Religion, Jewish. Proved same by producing circumcision. Amateur job, obviously work of apprentice mohel. Barak informed me fire caused by explosion natural gas. Twelve seventeen, radioed headquarters news of top-secret emergency." Kishner hesitated, wondering whether to mention Aunt Becky but then realized he would have to blow her cover as Hot Mama if he did so. He decided to keep his report crisp. "Twelve thirty-two, emergency units arrived. One four A.M., fire extinguished by large, controlled dynamite blast. One four and a half, neighboring pinochle game broke up. End of report." He closed his book snappily and sat down. Anyplace else in the world he would have clicked his heels.

"Well, gentlemen," said the Prime Minister, "those facts are only the tip of the iceberg. For the scientific explanation of this event, may I introduce Aluf Mordechai Haimowitz of the Defense Forces' Geological Survey Unit."

"Wait a minute!" Schoenbaum leaped to his feet. "Who is this Haimowitz? We got here an expert from Dallas, Texas, going to be my son-in-law, happens to be a Doctor of Oil. Chaim, stand up!"

Hesitantly, Harold got to his feet.

"Mr. Schoenbaum, General Haimowitz in civilian life is also the head of the Department of Geology at Hebrew University in Jerusalem." The Chief of State's smile was beginning to wear thin, but he still wore it bravely.

"So what is Chaim, chopped liver? He showed them where to drill one hole in Texas, came up so much oil, could have drowned Tel Aviv and Haifa together."

"Perhaps," said Aluf Mordechai Haimowitz, an un-military-looking professor with gold-rimmed eyeglasses, a graying beard and rumpled uniform, "since Mr. Barak-Bernstein was present at the inception, we might deliver a joint report." Haimowitz was uncomfortable outside his classroom unless he was carrying a rock hammer. At this moment he felt he could have used one. Failing that, his only hope was to get back to his laboratory as soon as possible. His military career was devoted entirely to avoiding conflict.

All eyes turned to Harold. He cleared his throat nervously. This was his opportunity to escape the Customs Service. He had to choose his words carefully.

"It has always seemed impossible to scientists," he said, "that only Israel, in the midst of the most fabulous underground reserves in the entire world, should be almost completely without petroleum."

"Correct!" encouraged Schoenbaum. "If God chose the Jews, it didn't occur to Him they would drive Cadillacs?"

"I have always felt," Harold continued, ignoring this assistance, "that under the considerable substratum of solid rock beneath much of Israel must lie the main source of the oil of the Middle East."

"May I add a comment?" asked Haimowitz, general, professor, and nebbish.

"Be my guest," said Harold magnanimously, warming to his role. There is something about addressing the upper levels of government that gives all who attain it the same euphoria as that which afflicts an aviator who reaches high altitude without sufficient oxygen. It is known in scientific terms as Anoxia, or Nixonia, depending on your political orientation.

"Thank you," said Haimowitz, grateful that Harold had given him a chance to get on. "We can only presume, since there has been no previous indication of such a structure in the millions of years of existence of the present landmass, that there must have been a recent catastrophic geological event that cracked the solid substratum and allowed the pressure from below to force the oil upward into the wide-open fissure."

"Schoenbaum, not Fisher!" shouted the old man, again. "Don't talk this way about a nice girl!"

Harold quickly covered for his future father-in-law by stepping into the startled pause with another observation. "There has been no recent geological event that can account for it," he asserted. "It is a complete mystery."

The Prime Minister coughed. He looked about him, trying to determine if this were the moment. Was he among friends? The Cabinet? Doubtful. Two of its members had already announced for his job. Schoenbaum? Not exactly a pillar of reliability. Haimowitz? A nebbish. But it was his duty as Prime Minister to present all the facts to those who had to make the fateful decisions. Eventually, they would have to know.

"Gentlemen," he said, "I must swear all of you to the

utmost secrecy. A few days ago, there was a slight error at the nuclear reactor at Dimona.''

There was a stir among his listeners. Most of them knew what was going on at the experimental reactor the nation was supposed to use solely to research new sources of energy. Did the world imagine that you could give a child who was being continually attacked by the kids next door a stick and a string and not have him fashion a bow and arrow? But in the convention of international hypocrisy about such matters, a convention that delivered atomic materials to India during its battle with Pakistan and announced the Indians were to use them to make watch dials that glowed in the dark, the real activities at Dimona had to be cloaked in pretense. Their leader was equal to the moment.

"Some fissionable material," he said slowly, so they would get his point, "accidentally fell out of its container and collected itself into the shape of a slight bomb, who knows how? It was an accident that could happen to anybody. It just happens that this slight bomb fell down into an oven built to bake cholent for the army. Cholent, as you know, is a kind of pot roast with potatoes and vegetables, which must bake for at least twenty-four hours before—"

"Twenty-six is better," said Schoenbaum. "My wife, God rest her soul, made it every Friday, if I wanted or I didn't want."

"Must bake for at least twenty-six hours," continued the Prime Minister, twitching slightly again. "We have a lot of men in the army, so it is a big oven. In fact, it was dug about three hundred feet underground, because with cholent you have to hold the heat in. So this slight bomb accidentally fell down on top of the cholent, the cholent was hot, and this slight bomb somehow managed to blow itself up. It just happens a lot of our army scientists were nearby, ready to sample the cholent to see if it was tasty enough for our boys, and they accidentally observed the results. It is my opinion that this geological event we have been talking about was the result of overcooking the cholent. And the slight underground explosion that accidentally happened may be what caused the underground oil to be forced upward into this wide-open—"

He saw Schoenbaum's look, and quickly changed course in midsentence.

"—into this crevice. Now, our little country is not supposed to have this kind of bomb, nor is it supposed to have oil. I'm not even certain we're allowed to have cholent, which can be lethal if not cooked twenty-six hours. So you can understand the necessity for complete secrecy. We believe President Carter of the United States is our friend, but we would not like him to ask for our reactor back so he can roast peanuts. You understand, of course, this is a joke. No disrespect is meant, since the CIA may have bugged this room."

Rov Aluf Kishner was on his feet.

"Mr. Prime Minister," he said, "we must prepare a cover story for what has happened. I suggest we report that the explosion and fire was caused when Jacob Schoenbaum left the gas on in his oven while preparing the food for the wedding of his daughter."

"Not so fast, sonny boy!" Schoenbaum was on his feet, instantly. "What am I, some kind cheapskate? Everybody in Tel Aviv knows it will be a catered affair. We might even have to postpone if that shlemiel in the Kikar Malchei—"

"Quiet!" The Prime Minister had reached the end of his tether. Gone was the politician. The commander in chief was speaking. "This is a matter of utmost urgency for your country, Fisher!"

"Schoenbaum."

Israel's leader twitched, again.

"Schoenbaum. The discovery of an oil deposit of this magnitude must be treated as a military secret so highly sensitive that any mention of it in the wrong place could cause a complete disruption of the delicate balance of power in the Middle East." He looked around the room at the Cabinet for confirmation. All of them nodded their approval, except the two who were running for his job, who shrugged. It was the closest to unanimity an Israeli Cabinet had ever achieved.

He pursued his advantage.

"All of you, every one of us in this room, must keep this completely secret under pain of instant imprisonment. Agreed?"

Nine ayes, two shrugs. Unanimous again.

"I want the solemn oath—"

"Excuse me," interrupted Haimowitz.

"Quiet! I want the solemn oath of all of you that because of urgent military necessity, no mention of the events of last night must ever be revealed. Not one whisper, not one hint, not one breath of—"

"Excuse me, sir, but outside, it's raining oil," Haimowitz whispered. He turned and pointed to the huge window of the penthouse, which was becoming streaked with a dark liquid. The Prime Minister crossed to it in one bound. Below, people were running around in the streets, the women covering their heads with babushkas. Some of the men had run into their homes and come out with pails, basins, tea kettles. One enterprising individual had opened the hood of his Toyota and placed a funnel in the oil intake. From the skies came a steady, black, sticky downpour.

The Cabinet gathered about the window. In the distance, from the vicinity of Chez Schoenbaum, an immense plume of oil was spurting hundreds of feet into the atmosphere.

Haimowitz cleared his throat apologetically. "I suggest," he murmured, "that instead of calling it the secret Schoenbaum Well, we refer to it from now on as the Pinsker Street Gusher."

The assembled Cabinet officials nodded in approval of the inevitable. Except for the two who shrugged.

"Gentlemen," said the Prime Minister, "secrecy has no place in a democracy. Since it is now absolutely unavoidable, I suggest that honesty is the best policy. International diplomacy may barely survive such a blow." He managed a small, honest smile. "We will tell the truth. Israel has made a major oil strike; a thousand barrels an hour must be shooting into the air from that wide-open Schoenbaum."

He strode to the door, twitching. The Cabinet meeting was over.

8 Schoenbaum Achieves Cabinet Rank

IT BEGAN AS a small ripple in a large pond. There were no headlines. A story on page three of the New York *Times* simply stated: "OIL STRIKE REPORTED IN TEL AVIV." An oil well, reportedly dug by accident, blew in with a roar last night and, after catching fire, blanketed part of the city of Tel Aviv with a coating of crude tar and residue. At times other wells have been tapped in the Holy Land, but in every case the deposits have been minor. It is anticipated this well is no exception. Geologists have long reported the substructure of Israel to be basically nonproductive, in direct contrast with the huge deposits in other areas of the Middle East."

The stock markets of the world took no notice. In Washington, President Carter was briefed on the development in a facetious note from the State Department: "Government of Israel reports oil strike. Our embassy indicates someone may have opened can of Portuguese sardines."

At the offices of Exxon, Gulf, Texaco, Shell, Atlantic-Rich-field, the Bank of America, and the Chase Manhattan, nothing interrupted the morning coffee break or the free Arabic lessons.

At the United Nations the General Assembly voted 144-0 that Israel should free all captured terrorists and return their weapons. There were no abstentions.

Only at 412 Hayarkon Street in the city of Tel Aviv, an unpretentious home in a residential district, was there any unusual activity. A delegation consisting of the chief of staff of the Israeli Defense Forces, the foreign minister, and the minister of the interior were paying a call on a somewhat homely woman, who was making them tea with lemon and handing out a few cookies. They had come to ask her to return to her old post as Prime Minister of the state of Israel.

"What for?" she inquired. "I like my new official position as an old Jewish lady much better. Try the ones with nuts, homemade, I'm baking again."

"You might as well know that our Premier is requesting it. He's afraid he'll have another breakdown."

The old Jewish lady, who used to spend her days and nights in the lonely job of fighting the whole world for her country, sighed wearily. She had heard the stories of their leader's nervous problems, caused in part by a mother who still called him daily to tell him how to run the country.

"What's so terrible now?" she inquired. "Nobody's attacking from the Sinai; they're not shooting rockets from the Golan; Kissinger isn't even in office. How much trouble can he be in?"

"Schoenbaum," said the chief of staff. "He is twitching from Schoenbaum."

When she looked puzzled, they explained it all to her. The oil well, the water bill, everything. Even Sonya's fissure.

"I don't understand," Golda said. "One man? That's the whole problem? Tell him to go back where he came from."

"That we can't do!" Berger, of the foreign ministry, reminded her. "That's what they tell everybody before they come here. That's what this country is here for."

"I know, I know," Golda told him wearily. "*We* have to take everybody. It's ruining the whole neighborhood."

The minister of the interior then explained the delicacy of the present situation. The Army Corps of Engineers, under the direction of Aluf Haimowitz—"That nudnik," remembered Golda—had dug some test holes in the area of the first well and come up with some startling data. The structure of the substrata had been cracked at only one point. There was no way to tap the huge underground pool except from the area of the rocky hillside that was entirely the property of Jacob Schoenbaum.

"Buy it from him," Mrs. Meir suggested. "Give him a nice profit, but not too nice. Then call me, I'll sell him some bonds."

"He won't sell at any price."

"Why not?"

"He's Schoenbaum."

"What does that mean?" the great old lady wanted to know.

The minister of the interior shrugged his shoulders—he was one of the shruggers. "You know the type. He's a tummler. He likes to tummel."

Tummeling is a procedure consisting of continuous activity and conflict, enjoyed immoderately by those who tummel. Genghis Khan was a tummler. Linda Lovelace is a tummler. Tummeling covers a wide area of human activity.

"All right, he wants to fight City Hall, condemn his property and take it for the army. We have the right."

"We don't want the enemy to know how big the oil deposit is. We don't want them to know how it came about. Most important, we don't want them to know about Dimona."

"So swear him to secrecy."

"Take a tummler's property away from him and expect him to shut up?"

Golda Meir understood. As Prime Minister she had run into the type. Too often.

"So arrest him," she said.

"In Israel? Arrest a Jew so we can take his property from him? Hitler is already laughing."

She knew she had no choice. She was the one who was always expected to solve the unsolvable.

"All right," she said, "I'm back, tell the Prime Minister to go to the mountains—we have a mountain now, Mount Hermon, remember? He should go to the mountains and rest. I'll take over for a while. And tell this Schoenbaum I want to talk to him right away. When it comes to tummeling, I am the head tummler."

The Israeli archives recording the events that followed have been burned. The feeling in government circles in Jerusalem was that they were better left in ashes. No future generation a millennium from now should find in the caves of Qumran another edition of the Dead Sea Scrolls delineating the shameful events leading to the establishment of the Pillar of Salt Playboy Club.

However, in the interest of history, much of the story has been pieced together from the secret files of the CIA, the FBI, the KGB, the PLO, and notes taken by the bartender at the Tel Aviv Waldorf-Astoria the night Jacob Schoenbaum polished off their stock of vintage slivovitz, after Sonya filed for divorce from Chaim-Harold.

It began routinely enough, once Golda Meir had taken over the reins of government, with a polite invitation to Schoenbaum to meet with the new Prime Minister in the house on Hayarkon Street. He went somewhat reluctantly. Mrs. Meir looked a lot like Sophie without lipstick, and the wound was too fresh. But he went. He was greeted with great warmth and respect. Golda took him by the arm, conducted him to the sofa, and personally poured each of them a nice scotch and water. Schoenbaum informed her he drank his scotch straight and told the Prime Minister what she could do with the water. Also with that shlemiel in the Kikar Malchei.

Mrs. Meir, who always made certain to be completely briefed on matters of state, patted the old man's arm.

"Schoenbaum," she said. "May I call you Schoenbaum?"

"What else?"

"Schoenbaum, that shlemiel in the Kikar Malchei has been fired."

"And my water bill?"

"You don't have to pay. Ever."

"And the water?"

"What do you expect, miracles? It still tastes terrible, but we're only charging half."

Schoenbaum reflected. It was a beginning, a sign of good faith. Also, he was being told the truth; no soft soap from Golda. He admired that, especially in a woman.

"So," said Schoenbaum, "you want something?"

"Naturally." Mrs. Meir was not one to beat about the bush. "Your house."

"It's gone," Schoenbaum reminded her. "Blown up by that farkockta cigar."

"Never mind," said the new Prime Minister. "The government would like to buy the hole where your house used to be."

"I'm an old man," Schoenbaum told her. "Money I don't need."

"Good!" Golda beamed. "Israel is a young country. Money we don't have."

"No wonder. You spent it all to build Miami Beach."

Mrs. Meir had been briefed on her visitor, but no mere briefing could do justice to the reality. In spite of her renowned talents as a peacemaker, she could feel her anger rising. But she knew she had to restrain herself; this little old man, who had just lighted that terrible cigar in her clean living room and was searching for an ashtray she knew he would never find in time to save her rug, was too important to the delicate political structure of this part of the world to be dealt with forthrightly. Under ordinary circumstances, she would have had him thrown bodily out of her home, but she knew her country couldn't afford that luxury. In a democratic nation, things must be done democratically. Golda Meir could only wish, wistfully, to be for a moment her neighbor the sultan of Oman, who amused himself by occasionally ordering a small public beheading.

Instead, she smiled at Schoenbaum.

"Naturally, we'll be more careful how we spend our budget in the future."

"More barbed wire, no more Fontainebleau hotels."

"Of course." Mrs. Meir forced herself to keep her mind on the fact that the old man who was putting his feet on her new inlaid coffee table controlled the most valuable oil reserves this side of the Red Sea.

"Listen, Schoenbaum," she said, "I'll put my cards on the table. We in Israel can't afford to confiscate private property like the Arabs do. We want to pay you a fair price. All I'm asking is that you name it."

"All I want," said Jacob Schoenbaum, who had been waiting for this moment all his life, "is I should be on the Cabinet."

Mrs. Meir choked on her drink. She didn't like scotch and had learned to drink it only because it was the international diplomatic currency, but it suddenly seemed more bitter than usual. She had expected to pay a high price for the Pinsker Street Gusher. But not this high.

"I'm sorry, no." Golda Meir was respected for her prompt decisions. Usually.

"Listen, Golda," said the old man, who was, after all, no older than she, "my son-in-law-to-be, he's a smart boy, he tells me you got to dig on my lot. All right, you want something, I want something. What I want is to holler on somebody. You know what this means?"

Golda nodded. It was her secret of governing.

"So," Schoenbaum continued, "since my Sophie, rest her soul, is gone, I got nobody in the house to holler on. I'm an old man. When I die, I want on my stone, 'He hollered on City Hall *and they listened.*' It's never happened before, *they had to listen.* I'll be the first. I want on the Cabinet. That's my final offer, take it or leave it.''

The army, Golda thought, tensely, they could take over the property under cover of darkness; if the old man resisted, maybe a submachine gun could go off accidentally. Then she sighed. No, that was the enemy's method. Schoenbaum had her against the wall.

''All right,'' said Mrs. Meir, knowing she would regret it. ''A Cabinet post. Minister of consumer affairs.''

''Wait,'' said Schoenbaum, ''there's more.''

''Oy,'' said the Prime Minister.

''The government should pay for the caterer for Sonya's wedding.''

''Done.''

''The hors d'oeuvres should be first class, the herring fresh.''

''First class. Fresh. I'll make a note. Maybe I'll make the herring myself.''

''If you don't mind, I prefer catered. Now the dowry I promised, ten thousand dollars, it would be nice if the government paid, not me.''

''Ten thousand?''

''Chaim-Harold wants a nice honeymoon, to rent a nice house; you think all this can be done with love?''

''Dowry, ten thousand. I made a note.''

''Also, there's going to be a company?''

''What company?''

''You can't have an oil well without you make a company. So Harold should be manager; you'll see he gets a nice salary.''

''I'm sure something can be arranged. Thank you, Schoenbaum, you and the state of Israel have a deal.'' Mrs. Meir held out her hand hopefully.

''There's more,'' said Schoenbaum, savoring the moment

and the Manuelo y Vega, which was dropping ashes on the carpet.

"I have an urgent call from Washington," said the Prime Minister. "Can you make it a little short?"

"Believe me, you got oil, Washington will hang on the line. What I want, you should get me another house."

"That's fair."

"Outside Tel Aviv, in Savyon. The one looks like the White House. It's my style. Aso, it would be nice Sonya got married in the White House rose garden."

Mrs. Meir groaned. It would be difficult and expensive to get the eccentric Iranian millionaire who had insisted on building an exact duplicate of the Washington White House in a suburb of Tel Aviv out of his strange obsession. But there seemed to be no alternative.

"All right," she said, and held out her hand again.

"There's more," said Schoenbaum.

"Naturally." Golda was getting to know her man.

"This is the most important. Schoenbaum pays no taxes the rest of his life, and also nothing to the UJA; you got enough hotels."

Mrs. Meir hesitated. The entire basis of a democracy was being challenged. Power existed in the ability of a government to get the taxpayer to vote to continue taxing himself. The freedom to pay taxes is fundamental in a republic. Further, in a Jewish state with the heaviest tax load in the world, the voter is also expected to pledge whatever he has left to an infinite number of Jewish charities. Otherwise, he might spend his income foolishly on food and shelter. Money for food and shelter is to be secured from the tourists, not from the government. To exempt one citizen from these responsibilities might provoke revolution, especially if that citizen were Schoenbaum, who couldn't be expected to shut up about it.

"No," said Golda firmly.

Schoenbaum got to his feet and found his derby. He flicked the ashes from his cigar on the rug again.

"Okay by me," he said. "Bring over the army, throw me out, an old man seventy-five years old, goes to temple every Shabbas—how will this look in the United Nations?"

The Prime Minister knew only too well. Unanimous vote of censure. Give back the captured territory. Kissinger might be sent over again, even though he was no longer secretary of state. It wasn't worth the risk.

She took Schoenbaum's hand in hers.

"A deal," she said. Unconditional surrender.

"A deal," Schoenbaum said.

When Schoenbaum gave his word, it was done.

Prime Minister Golda Meir presented the news to the Knesset, gathered in secret session the next day.

"The nation of Israel," she declared, "for so long isolated by friend and foe alike, has discovered the greatest friend of all. No election can change this friendship; no vote can force us to give it back; no ally can cut our throats while this friend is on our side. When God told Moses to lead the children of Israel into the land of milk and honey, it is clear now that he meant the land of milk, honey, and Mobilgas. Our scientists tell us the Pinsker Street Gusher has tapped an underground source of oil estimated to equal that of the entire Persian Gulf."

There was a startled whisper in the chamber. Everyone knew of the strike; no one knew it was of such immense proportions.

"We have now drilled eleven wells in the area," the Prime Minister continued. "And I am happy to tell you there isn't a dry hole in the entire fissure."

"Schoenbaum!" shouted an angry old voice from the back of the chamber, and Mrs. Meir cursed her stupidity in allowing the new Cabinet to attend the session.

"Obviously," she continued bravely, "the oil supply far exceeds this tiny nation's needs. Obviously, we would like

9 You Can Trust Your Car to the Man Who Wears the Star

THE BOARDROOM of the Texaco Corporation is located on the thirty-sixth floor of the Texaco Building in downtown Dallas. It is a huge room paneled in expensive walnut, with deep pile rugs, a crystal chandelier, and a huge table around which sit the directors of the American branch of an international oil corporation so rich, so powerful it resisted for a full half day, including lunch, the efforts of little Saudi Arabia to nationalize Texaco's oil fields. Like all the American members of the international consortium known as Aramco, it participated in the oil boycott with the Arab nations by refusing to supply oil from its reserves to the American Seventh Fleet in the Mediterranean, arguing that since the Seventh Fleet was not going to attack Saudi Arabia to get back its property, as it would certainly have done in the days of Teddy Roosevelt, Texaco's patriotic responsibilities to the U.S. of A. were limited to trying to avoid paying taxes.

The colossus of the oil business had called its directorate together because of the rumors of new developments in the

Middle East. Its political department, a little-known wing of the company that maintains its own intelligence service, had passed along information that made it necessary for Texaco to prepare for some international sidestepping. A corporation like Texaco is engaged in several simultaneous chess games, involving many nations and many competing giants in the oil business, and psychological warfare has become an important part of the profit picture. Texaco had gotten a huge jump on its competitors in the early days of the development of the Arab oil reserves when its then-president, a shrewd and intuitive leader, had been the first to have the table in the boardroom rearranged so that he faced Mecca. The gesture had not gone overlooked, by either the rulers of the oil sheikhdoms or the president of Exxon, who then planned to place a copy of the Koran in every rest room of every Exxon service station. Fortunately, cooler heads prevailed.

Pembroke Sheaffer, the newly elected president of the Texaco Corporation, called the board meeting to order, after the usual brief prayer offering thanks to Allah for that month's business. He immediately got down to brass tacks.

"Gentlemen," he said, "we have an opportunity to get the jump on our competition in a completely unfair way, which is completely fair because if they had our information first, they would do it to us."

There was general approval around the table. "Screw unto others as they would screw unto you." The language was unfortunate, but that sentiment had been the cornerstone of big business since the first successful patent infringement at the time of the invention of the wheel. No one remembers the name of the wheel's inventor, but everyone knows the emblem of the Rotary Club.

"We have learned of a secret speech by the Prime Minister of Israel to her Parliament, claiming the discovery of oil reserves in the Holy Land. We have also learned to discount the claims of the Israelis, which as you know is the only discount this company gives, but we have our own intelligence sources operating in the higher levels of that country's government. I must swear you to secrecy on this point, as it could expose a very large covert operation."

He paused, meaningfully. The board decided, in their own minds, that Texaco, quite properly, had a few hundred secret agents operating in Jerusalem and Tel Aviv. How could they know that the large covert operation was Nadya Haffaz? Nadya, by means known only to herself and the two Cabinet ministers who did not shrug her off—in fact, were they inclined to, they probably did not have the strength—had secured some pertinent data. The fact that it had been planted by Shimon Gan and Israeli intelligence did not make it less valid; sometimes the truth makes the best propaganda, but only when it appears someone is trying to hide it.

"We have the geological information we need to interpret the Israeli claims," President Sheaffer continued. "The size of the oil pool beneath the Pinsker Street Gusher is truly astronomical. It seems quite probable that if we can gain its control, we can tell that shlemiel in Saudi Arabia what he can do with our expropriated property." He was, of course, referring to King Khalid, but the situation was too delicate to mention him by name. It was too early to be certain the Israeli reserves would prove out, and the king might still be important, in spite of the antipathy the expropriation had provoked. It was like the old Hollywood saying, "I'll never use that son of a bitch again until I need him."

But King Khalid might not be needed. The seismological soundings taken by the Haimowitz unit of the Israeli Defense Forces indicated a possible reserve of over fifteen billion barrels. It might be the largest deposit yet recorded on the face of the globe. Before the information reached the hands of its competitors, Texaco had to move fast. It also had to make certain the government of Israel would regard it in a more favorable light than in the past.

It was a momentous occasion. The international oil industry was approaching a crucial crossroad, and Texaco had reached it first. The die had been cast; the fatal decision had been made. All that remained was the formality of the approval by the board of directors. Sheaffer's voice trembled, but his resolve never wavered. What was good for Texaco was good for the United States, wasn't it? Sheaffer was not a very original thinker, but he was certainly in the mainstream.

"Gentlemen!" His voice rang out across the paneled boardroom. "On the advice of our psychological tactics division, I wish to announce a change in the Texaco emblem!"

With the practiced theatricality of the born salesman, Pembroke Sheaffer pulled the curtain that had concealed the huge billboard on the wall behind his chair.

There was a startled gasp from the assembled board of directors.

"Our new trademark!" the president announced, proudly. "We have purchased all rights from Mogen David wine!"

The famous Texaco Star now had six points.

There was stunned silence, shock, and then a wave of applause for this daring move on the part of the new president, who in one quantum leap had left Shell Oil and its seashell emblem high on the beach.

Shellfish are not kosher.

It had never mattered before.

The White House Wedding, Savyon style, of Chaim-Harold Barak-Bernstein and Sonya Fisher-Schoenbaum was the social event of the Tel Aviv season. It was held in the rose garden, as Schoenbaum had stipulated, and the turnout of friends, pinochle players, and government officialdom was of sufficient size to swamp the caterer, who sent out an all-points bulletin for more herring before the affair was half over. The herring had to be fresh, but since this fish is not indigenous to the Mediterranean, the Red Sea, or the Persian Gulf, it must be imported into Israel by air. It seems incredible the Lord overlooked this point when he distributed his creatures over the face of the earth. Israel has no national bird, no national flower, but if it had a national fish, it would have to be imported from Greece, where they don't even like it.

Also, the wedding was held during a chumsin. This is the hot wind that blows into the small country from the desert during the summer and turns the usually unbearable climate into one that is unthinkable. There is an unwritten law that no one can be convicted for a murder committed during the chumsin. The reason it is unwritten is that no one can write during the chumsin, and no judge could wear a robe during that heat. The trouble with the unwritten law is that during a chumsin it is too hot to bother to kill anyone, so most murderers let their big chance slip by.

None of this bothered Schoenbaum, for whom this moment was the culmination of all the hopes and dreams he and Sophie had shared from the moment Sonya had been born: His daughter was being married at a catered affair, and she was wearing a beautiful white wedding gown, white testifying to her virginal purity, the perspiration beading her pretty forehead caused only in part by the chumsin, the rest by her conscience. The garden behind the Savyon White House was crawling with perspiring dignitaries: The Prime Minister herself had come from a Cabinet meeting with the entire Cabinet; the ambassadors of the United States, Great Britain, France, Germany, and Italy had brought wedding gifts to prove their countries' regard for Schoenbaum and their lack of oil reserves.

Uncle Zvi was much in evidence; he had arranged the Savyon White House sale to the government and its transfer to Schoenbaum. This was no pea patch transaction; the size of the price had Texas overtones. Only Schoenbaum's insistence on tradition had prevented Uncle Zvi from turning the wedding into a barbecue—tradition and the absence of sufficient quantities of pork ribs and chitlins. Uncle Zvi served as best man, ushering Harold down the garden path to meet his blushing bride, blushing because she and Harold had earlier been surprised by the bridesmaids in the Lincoln bedroom, where

Harold had been instructing her in the Emancipation Proclamation.

Now Sonya took his hand as they stood together under the wedding canopy and the watchful eye of the rabbi, who was intoning the sacred ceremony in Hebrew. The rabbi offered them each a drink from a crystal wineglass, then threw it to the ground and Harold crushed it under his heel in the traditional manner, causing the rabbi to suffer a slight flesh wound on his ankle because he had removed his socks for the duration of the chumsin.

If only Sophie could be here to see this, thought Schoenbaum, trying with difficulty to blink back the tears. She hated rabbis. But she loved weddings. And she loved Sonya. So now, together, Sophie and Schoenbaum had brought their little girl safely to the port of marriage, scraping her bottom only slightly on the voyage; now, thought Schoenbaum, he could at last relax and devote himself to hollering on the government, from his new vantage point in the Cabinet. He looked at Sonya fondly as the ring was being slipped on her finger. "Home is the sailor, home from the sea," he thought, and looked at Harold, "and the hunter home from the hill," Schoenbaum concluded. Had he remembered that Robert Louis Stevenson had written those lines as his obituary, he might have been forewarned, but so absorbed was he by the ritual he didn't even notice that Harold was having difficulty in finding Sonya's finger because nearby the shapely secretary to the French ambassador had loosened her blouse because of the heat and created a personal chumsin of her own.

Golda Meir watched the ceremony with mixed emotions; she hoped the children would be happy, but she knew from her own experience it takes more than a rabbi to make a marriage. It was so long ago that Golda had been young; it was so long ago that her marriage had interfered with her career; it was so long ago that she had agonized between love and duty, and duty had won. Science had learned how to freeze everything but youth. Maybe, Golda thought, it was a good thing.

The French ambassador, Pierre Alfonse Duplessis, had moved to her side as the ceremony concluded and everyone began to attack the hors d'oeuvres and the Carmel wine. The ambassador was a wise, ambitious representative of a nation that had been alternately Israel's best friend and foremost foe, as the political and economic winds blew. The winds were shifting again, and he hastened to be the first to assume a new tack.

"Madame Prime Minister," he breathed, kissing her hand—the one that wasn't occupied with a cracker topped with chopped liver. "France is so happy for you and your people."

"Yes," said Golda, "to have a boy and girl who want to get married, it's certainly a mitzvah today."

"I mean more than that, madame," said the ambassador. "My country would be delighted to be Israel's friend and ally again. Oh, not because of the oil—no, no, our friendship goes much deeper, although your oil is also deep, no?"

He smiled at her. The purpose of diplomatic conversation is to achieve everything by indirection. But not with Golda.

"Listen, Lucky Pierre," she said, "you want oil, fine. But don't tell me who's our friend. What happened when you had Abu Daoud, the man who planned a new event for the Munich Olympics, in your hands? How could you give an assassin a free ticket on Air France to take him to Algiers first class? Tourist wasn't good enough?"

"A misunderstanding," he purred. "We thought he was Omar Sharif."

"It didn't have anything to do with the billion dollars' worth of planes you were getting ready to sell Egypt?"

"Nonsense. The government of France would not compromise its integrity for the price of a few meals at the Tour d'Argent."

"I'd like to believe that."

"I have been empowered to inform you that whatever La Belle France can do to prove our friendship will be done, *tout de suite.*"

"Fine," said Golda, "how about La Belle France importing ten thousand cases of Israeli champagne?"

There was a shocked silence.

"Israeli champagne? In *France?*"

"French warplanes? In *Egypt?*"

The ambassador drew himself up. "Madame Meir," he said, "this is not a matter for levity. I am offering you the sincere friendship of my government. In our hearts, we have always been Israel's friend."

"Never mind in your hearts, how about in the United Nations?"

"You are not going to base our friendship on what a sovereign nation decides is its best interest in an international tribunal? We need oil from many sources."

"An eye for an eye, a tooth for a tooth, a barrel for a vote in the General Assembly. Israel also operates by divine inspiration, but we've been doing it longer. *Au 'voir, monsieur l'ambassadeur.*"

And she turned away, enjoying the chopped liver. And the warm Israeli champagne. And the new experience of being courted. It was, she knew, only the beginning. Genesis. And she thought again about the strange news she had received the morning before the wedding from her foreign minister, Abba Eban, who had been returned to his old post to the great joy of Schoenbaum, who liked to think ahead. If Harold for some reason should drop dead one day, he wanted his next choice for Sonya's hand and adjoining anatomy to have a steady job.

Eban had told the prime minister he had been contacted through discreet diplomatic channels by representatives of the Saudi Arabian government. They wished to send a dignitary to attend the Schoenbaum-Bernstein nuptials and wanted a safe-conduct pass into Israel across the Allenby Bridge from the west bank of the Jordan. It was, as Yul Brynner once said, a puzzlement. But the permission had been granted. Mrs. Meir was now waiting curiously to see what purpose lay behind the strange request from the country's mortal enemy. She knew, from Shimon Gan and Israeli intelligence, that a vehicle had been escorted across the bridge several hours ago and was well on its way to the Savyon White House.

She was aroused from her reverie by the loud voice of Jacob Schoenbaum, tummeling with the photographers about what was the best angle to photograph Sonya and Harold, in fond embrace, for the wedding album. Golda smiled to herself. Secretly she admired the contumelious old man. He had taken on the government of Israel single-handedly and had done far better than France and her entire diplomatic corps.

By this time Harold Barak-Bernstein was finding the continuous embrace with a yielding Sonya, here in the hot sun of the chumsin, almost unbearable.

"Let's get out of here quickly," he whispered in her ear as they kissed for the photographers for the twentieth time, "or we're liable to have our whole honeymoon in front of the cameras."

"Shhh," she whispered, as eager as he. The earth hadn't moved for either of them for a month since Sonya had been so busy preparing the wedding and the quarters her father had arranged for them in the Savyon White House. "We can't leave yet."

But she pressed against him, and Chaim-Harold suddenly lifted her off her feet and started to run with her toward the front of the White House, through laughing and applauding guests, toward the driveway. There the four-door Mercedes awaited, a gift Schoenbaum had arranged from a grateful and pained government, decorated now with Hebrew "Just Married!" signs, or, more correctly since the language runs from right to left, Hebrew "!deirraM tsuJ" signs. The happy couple's path was suddenly blocked by a huge Silver Cloud Rolls-Royce, which drew to a halt in front of them. A white-robed Arab driver climbed out and crossed to the rear door, which he opened with a flourish, and then bowed low.

Out of the rear of the Rolls-Royce stepped a distinguished dark Arab with a clipped beard, wearing a silken burnoose flecked with gold thread. He was carrying a small envelope. He inclined his head toward Harold and to Sonya, still clutched in Harold's arms, as the guests drew closer, mystified.

"I am Mustapha Ben al-Harout," he said in a precise British-trained accent, "Foreign minister of the kingdom of Saudi Arabia. I bring an offering of friendship to Chaim-Harold Barak and his bride from His Royal Majesty King Khalid." He extended the envelope to the startled couple. "Take it," he said. "You will find inside a gift certificate for an expensive washer and dryer."

And he bowed and kissed Sonya's hand.

It was indeed a puzzlement.

That night, in Jerusalem, Shimon Gam was reporting another strange development to the Prime Minister, in the government offices near the Knesset. The friendly eye-in-the-sky satellite of the United States had again involuntarily provided Israeli intelligence with startling new photographs.

The white dots were disappearing from the Golan Heights and the Sinai. Plan B was being discontinued. The tank menace to Israel's security was Gone with the Chumsin.

Mrs. Meir and her chief of intelligence puzzled over the day's surprising evidence.

"It can't be our oil," the Prime Minister decided. "They have much more than we have. Perhaps it was the explosion in the cholent oven; they may have gotten wind of that."

"That might explain the withdrawal of the tanks," Shimon agreed, "but what explains the expensive washer and dryer?"

"You think Schoenbaum is dealing with Saudi Arabia behind our backs?"

"Schoenbaum and the Arabs? Never. They'd tummel each other to death."

"Shimon," said Golda, "you've got to get us more information. From within enemy territory. From the palace itself, if possible."

"What would you suggest?"

"Nadya Haffaz."

General Shimon Gan shook his head sadly.

"Wouldn't work," he said. "King Khalid is a very thin, very slight old man; she'd suffocate him."

"He might mumble something important before he went."

"What would he want with Nadya? He's got a harem of forty beautiful women. They work in shifts around the clock. Why do you think the king is so thin?"

"All right. Maybe Nadya was a bad idea. But there must be other, less exotic ways."

"I'll put Shemuhl Kishner on it. Maybe he can bug the bedrooms of the king's wives."

"With forty concubines, when would Khalid get around to one of his wives?"

"That's just it. The wives must be getting around a little on their own. Wouldn't you, if your husband had been playing around with forty other women?"

"I'm an old Jewish lady; it's difficult to remember," said Golda Meir. "Besides, I was so busy in the government."

"If we can get evidence on only one or two wives," Shimon told her, "we can put pressure on them to get us the information we need from the king."

"How will they get it if they don't see him?"

"He must come out of the harem sometime. Maybe between meals."

"And how will they get information from him?"

"They'll cry."

The Prime Minister considered that. It might work. In more than five thousand years it always had.

She gave her chief of intelligence her approval. All systems were Go.

Except in the honeymoon suite of the Caesarea Hotel, where certain of the new Mrs. Chaim-Harold Barak's systems were Stop.

10 How Do You Get a Jewish Girl to Stop?

THE ROMAN CITY of Caesarea is the most romantic spot in all Israel. It is located some sixty kilometers and twenty centuries from modern Tel Aviv, its ancient Roman ruins and amphitheater surrounding a sparkling blue Mediterranean bay. Where else but in the honeymoon suite of the Caesarea Hotel could you overlook the Herod Stables and Riding School, sipping a cooling Julius Caesar cocktail, as you watched the moonlit shadows on the crumbling fortress where, in 66 A.D., the Roman legions played mumblety-peg on the bodies of whatever Jewish prisoners happened to be stretched out on the rack? This archaic practice was discontinued for more than two thousand years, until it was figuratively revived recently in New York City in the United Nations' little games with Israel.

Chaim-Harold Bernstein was undergoing similar exquisite torture at the hands of his bride of only a few hours. They had wandered, hand in hand, over the moonlit white sand of the lovely beach and the picturesque Crusader ruins for almost a full three minutes before Harold dragged Sonya into the hotel and up to their bedroom. She had protested that there were many more sights to be seen, including what the guidebooks described as "the only real, live golf course in Israel," but her husband was not interested in breaking par that night, merely equaling it. He couldn't understand the sudden change in his inamorata, who had provided him with several interesting previews of the next forty-three years during the period before the wedding while the Pinsker Street oilfield was being expanded and both of them might have died from lack of enjoyment.

To Harold's sorrow, he had never heard the joke that is as old as Caesarea itself: How do you get a Jewish girl to stop fucking? Marry her.

Not that Sonya had stopped completely; only, as mentioned before, certain systems. These systems of pleasure have been referred to in the past by the names of great nations: Greece, France, Italy. But no one, you may have noted, has ever suggested to his mate in a moment of reckless passion, "Let's do it Jewish style." It doesn't exist, because a Jewish Princess, once the marriage vows have been performed and she is no longer required to lure a male to the altar or her mother will drop dead, immediately finds it necessary to endure only the minimum of conjugal duties that will allow her to keep the franchise. No matter that she and Harold were truly in love; no matter that, before marriage, they had thrilled to a variety of experiences. After the ceremony any departure from the simple horizontal found her in the grip of a migraine headache.

Sonya, wild, gay Sonya, had suddenly become Mrs. Chaim Barak, Jewish nun, defender of woman's rights in the bedroom, moral leader of the community, president of the PTA, never on Sunday, never on Shabbas, sometimes on Wednesday, and once in a while Monday afternoon if there was nothing good on daytime television. Since, in Israel, there is no daytime television, Chaim-Harold Barak-Bernstein was going to have to find himself a hobby.

Fortunately, he didn't know this at the time. He could not

foresee the bleak sexual future with a Jewish Princess who would, traditionally, descend from the throne only to allow her husband to kiss her feet and nothing else. Except Wednesdays.

"Darling," he whispered tenderly. "Please."

"No."

"But we're married!"

"You shouldn't expect a married woman to do such things."

"Why not? I learned from married women when I was fourteen years old and had a paper route."

"You're not going to deliver any papers here. Besides, I have a terrible headache."

He kissed her behind the left ear. There are not many women who can resist a kiss behind the left ear, headache or no. It stirred memories in Sonya, memories of the carefree girl she used to be, and suddenly, in violation of all Jewish Princesshood, she found herself turning to her husband as if he were still her lover, and soon they were as happy as if the ceremony had never been performed, and then the telephone rang.

"Don't answer it," whispered Sonya, but since she wasn't facing Chaim-Harold at that moment, he didn't even hear her. He sat up with a groan. He had remembered that he was general manager of the Pinsker Street Oil Conglomerate, and from now on he always had to answer the telephone.

He picked up the receiver.

"Barak here," he said sharply. "Make it snappy, this is a honeymoon."

"Chaim! We need you right away!"

He recognized the anguished voice of Aluf Mordechai Haimowitz. He also recognized Sonya's anguished voice. Never start anything you can't finish, he reminded himself, and was about to hang up when Haimowitz's next words froze him at the telephone.

"The pressure in the wells is building instead of dropping," said the military nebbish. "Three wells we were still digging suddenly blew in; all of a sudden we have gushers all over. I'm in a telephone booth; already the oil is up to my ankles, ruined my Bass Weejuns. Come over here quick!''

"I told you, I'm on my honeymoon!''

"This is urgent; we hit one well only four feet down; maybe we should build an ark!''

"Darling," breathed Sonya. "*My* pressure is building, too."

Harold hesitated. From the way the evening had begun, it might be a good idea for Sonya to build up a little pressure for the future.

"I shall be there as soon as humanly possible," he announced in his managerial voice. "Take some accurate seismological readings."

"And you," said Aluf Mordechai Haimowitz, scientist, "better bring a towel, this stuff stains." And he hung up, his Weejuns beyond repair.

Harold was already out of bed, getting into his pants. Sonya had climbed back and pulled the sheet up about her.

"Is this what our married life is going to be like?" she inquired, pouting. "Every night you run off to sit up with a sick oil well?"

"I have an idea," Chaim informed her, "the oil wells will go away as soon as your headaches do."

And he kissed her good-bye and left, master of his fate, captain of his soul. For one night.

Which, as marriages to Jewish Princesses go, is a pretty good average.

The area around the Pinsker Street Gusher had changed dramatically since Schoenbaum's Well had first blown in. The entire hillside was a mass of oil derricks and machinery, pipelines running to storage tanks, makeshift sheds and buildings, drilling rigs boring continuously into the rock and the seemingly endless wealth below. Tanker trucks, jeeps, a spur of the little Israel Railroad, and hundreds of hard-bitten oilfield workers, some imported from Chaim's native Texas, swarmed over the tangled area that was illuminated constantly with floodlights. The black gold was everywhere, spewing from the gushers, gurgling from the pipelines, fouling the air and spreading over the surface of the ground to a height of several inches over the plank sidewalks. It was a noisy, slam-bang, boom town atmosphere. One expected to see Clark Gable and Spencer Tracy, their faces streaked with oil, bellowing orders to the drillers as another gusher spun in and the girls lined up in front of the dance hall so the hundred-dollar bills could be stuffed more easily into their bodices or whatever was handy.

But instead of Gable and Tracy, it was Haimowitz and Barak, huddled over a seismograph in a little shack at one corner of the field. The Hebrew lettering on a sign over the entrance read: ''.QH etaremolgnoC liO treetS reksniP.'' Chaim's eyes grew wider as he fed figures into a computer input and stared in disbelief as the results became visible on the video display. The little nation had made its most modern facilities available to the Pinsker Street operation. The complex mathematical computations were actually being carried out over special lines connecting the shack to the huge Intel computer bank in Beersheba at Ben-Gurion University, named for David Ben-Gurion *after* he was dead and buried, of course.

Chaim turned to Haimowitz. "If these figures are accurate," he said, "we have to present them to the highest government authorities immediately, preferably within the hour!"

"Don't be silly," said Aluf Haimowitz. "It's the middle of the night; how can you get the government together so quick?"

But Chaim was already dialing the phone. "Pop?" he said. "It's Sonny Boy. Holler on Golda."

The problem with Israel is that the country is so small, when a meeting is called within the hour it is almost impossible not to be able to get to it. That is, if the government is willing to put a Piper Cub at your disposal. The Piper is the basic trainer for the Israeli air force. Most of the army, including the women soldiers, know how to get one off the ground, sometimes by pushing. Since the turning radius of most jet aircraft is larger than the boundaries of the country in many places, the Piper is the safest way to get from one point in Israel to another without passing over Jordan, Syria, or Lebanon, which are not covered by flight insurance. So when Golda received Schoenbaum's imperative holler over her private phone, she could be assured the entire Cabinet could be assembled at the Tel Aviv Hilton in less time than it took Gerald Ford to get from Washington, D.C., to Dulles Airport on January 20, 1977.

There was a great deal of grumbling from the Cabinet ministers, especially from the two who had been spending the night with Nadya Haffaz. Even Golda, who had been assured by Schoenbaum this was a genuine emergency, was not certain the meeting was absolutely necessary. She had acted on intuition; Schoenbaum himself didn't understand the reason for the meeting, but if it helped make his son-in-law important and maybe raise his salary, it was okay by Schoenbaum.

"My son-in-law, the Doctor of Oil, wants to tell us about a big discovery he just made," the old man declared to the assembled Cabinet, only a little worried because Chaim had left Sonya alone in the honeymoon bed. General Haimowitz, seated beside Chaim, cleared his throat meaningfully until Schoenbaum noticed him.

"Oh, yes," the old man added, "this was a joint discovery with Aluf Nebbish."

Haimowitz nodded, satisfied. His contribution had been recognized.

Chaim-Harold got to his feet and walked to a blackboard on which he had chalked a geological map.

"Gentlemen," he said, picking up a pointer and indicating the blackboard, "this is a diagram of the Pinsker Street substrata, extracted from information just secured this evening from new seismological soundings and data processing in the Intel computer. It seems that when the accident in the cholent oven caused the rock structure to shift, it opened up this huge underground Schoenbaum that extends for miles, deep beneath the surface.''

There was no need to translate. The word ''Schoenbaum'' had taken its place in the fabric of the language, along with shlimazl, nebbish, and momzer. It meant any wide opening. Sonya was now immortal.

''With the drilling of so many wells, the pressure above the Schoenbaum suddenly dropped, creating a vacuum. This, in turn, caused a breakthrough in the rock structure around here''—he indicated an area with his pointer—''and the rush of a tremendous amount of previously untapped oil to fill the Schoenbaum. This oil poured in so quickly it reversed the pressure trend, eventually building to the point where it burst through to the surface in wells that were only half dug.'' Chaim-Harold was becoming more and more professorial, a role he was beginning to enjoy. He wondered if, in his new job, he might insist on tenure.

''Chaim,'' said Golda, ''I'm an old Jewish lady. Get to the point before I get a lot older.''

''All right,'' said Harold, only slightly miffed. He had intended to drag out his big moment for at least another fifteen minutes, but he could see he was beginning to lose his audience, two of whom had already wandered to the phone to call Nadya and tell her to put another bottle of slivovitz on ice.

''Where does this tremendous amount of new oil come from?'' He paused dramatically.

''It's your honeymoon night,'' said Schoenbaum. ''You would rather play Twenty Questions?''

''I will tell you the answer,'' Harold continued, since he had no choice. It was an answer, he knew, that was a political bombshell, an economic hot potato. After this announcement,

Arab complacency would vanish; they might even be compelled to sell that symbol of Arab culture, the London Dorchester Hotel.

"Now hear this," Chaim declared, cleverly milking the last second of suspense. "Our calculations indicate that the underground Schoenbaum lies at a greater depth than all the other major oil deposits in the Middle East. Therefore, they all are draining into the area under Pinsker Street. I would deduce that this is already lowering the pressure in oilfields from Benghazi to Teheran, from Abu Dhabi to Riyadh."

"The washer and dryer!" cried Golda as it all became clear to her. "That shlemiel in Saudi Arabia is in trouble! Get me Shimon Gan on the hot line!"

The Cabinet meeting broke up in an excited babble of conjecture. The economic tables were turning. Could diplomacy be far behind? The nation of Israel was entering a new phase. The Prime Minister would soon issue a decree: Stop the wailing at the Wailing Wall! The Shah of Iran had offered to finance the mortgage on a new temple!

But all this was still in the future. First came Golda's conversation on the hot line with Aluf Shimon Gan.

"Send Shemuhl Kishner into Saudi Arabia; let him bug a few bedrooms in the palace; we must know if King Khalid is having heartburn," the Prime Minister ordered. "We have to double-check the evidence from the Pinsker Street Gusher."

"Not necessary," Shimon informed Mrs. Meir crisply. "We just intercepted a radio message from the Foreign Office in Riyadh to the headquarters of the Arab League in Tripoli, Libya. It contains only three words, but we believe they are significant."

"What are the three words?"

" 'Up Shit Creek.' "

"Sounds encouraging," said Golda. "If I wasn't a nice old Jewish lady, I'd say we had them by the balls."

"What do we do next?"

"What else? Enjoy!"

And she hung up, humming happily to herself for the first time since 1947, when King Ibn Saud, Khalid's predecessor, had issued a call to a Holy War: "There are fifty million Arabs. What does it matter if we lose ten million to kill all the Jews? The price is worth it."

The price was getting higher. Inflation had mercifully set in.

Yaakov Ari Dunin strode across the tremendously impressive arc formed by the columns of Bernini as the bells in the huge dome of St. Peter's tolled midday. It was only September, but a chill breeze was sending the spray from the fountain in the center of Piazza San Pietro across the cobblestones of the ancient square, forerunner of another of Rome's damp and freezing winters. April in Paris, Autumn in New York, how come I get assigned to Chilblains in Rome? he thought to himself. Dunin had only recently taken up his post as Israel's representative to the Italian government. He had a reputation as a troubleshooter, and he knew by the time spring rolled around and the Roman evenings became soft and seductive, he would be in charge of purchasing several shiploads of fertilizer in Tegucigalpa, Honduras.

His mother was so happy he was in the diplomatic service. How would she feel now, knowing he had been summoned to the Holy See for an audience with His Holiness Pope Paul VI? A Nice Jewish Boy named Yaakov Dunin going to meet a fellow who lived upstairs from a church!

"You couldn't get him to come to the office?" he could hear his mother saying.

"No, Mama, he's an old man. It's better I go to him."

"But it's only a week before Rosh Hashonah; he couldn't wait till after the holidays?"

"It's an important matter; we don't have representation at the Vatican; this is special; it can't wait."

"Whatever you do, don't walk inside the church; God could

strike you dead. And after you see the Pope, wash your hands.''

''Yes, Mama.''

Dunin smiled. In his imaginary conversations with his mother, he never won an argument, just as in reality. But it made him feel better.

He presented his credentials to the Swiss Guard at the barrier, marveling that Michelangelo not only designed a uniform that made hardened soldiers look like circus clowns, but actually took credit for it. The guard seemed surprised that the Israeli ambassador had arrived on foot, instead of in a limousine. How could Dunin explain that the Israeli limousine—actually a Fiat 131—had a broken crankshaft and was in the garage for repairs, the garage was on strike, and the Israeli embassy had no budget for hiring a second limousine? A practical man, the ambassador had taken the bus. He had heard all the wild rumors floating around about the Israeli oil strike, he had been informed of the Prime Minister's speech, but he had a feeling it was all a diplomatic ploy, like almost everything else in life. So far, the rumors had not materialized in hard cash in the diplomatic pouch; until that moment, Dunin, like most of his countrymen, would remain a skeptic.

As he was ushered down the rococo hallways that had not changed since the days of the Renaissance, beneath such splendors of mosaic and paint and gold and silver as made his own government's modest offices in Jerusalem look like a junkie's bedroom, he wondered why the Pontiff wanted to speak to a representative of Israel. The last time it had happened was several years back, when Pope Paul gave an audience to Golda Meir. Nothing much had come of that, although Golda had sold him a bond. A small one. Yaakov Dunin felt today's meeting would have even less success. He could not help remembering that Pius XII had played footsie with the Nazi occupiers of Rome, for reasons never adequately explained to the B'nai B'rith.

He was ushered into the ornate chamber that served as the

private office of the Holy Father and hesitated as the slight figure in the scarlet robe and slippers rose to greet him some-what stiffly, as if his back were hurting. Those crazy red shoes, Dunin thought; he really wears them. Was he supposed to kiss the ring? Should he kneel? How far did protocol force him to deny his religion? He prayed for some inspiration as the white-haired priest with the gold-rimmed spectacles and the crucifix hanging about his neck on a gold chain slowly ap-proached him. The sight of the crucifix mesmerized Ambas-sador Dunin. The symbol of a religion that had altered the world, he thought. He suddenly wondered what would have happened if Pontius Pilate had ordered Jesus to the electric chair instead of the cross; would the Pope be wearing a little gold electric chair around his neck?

His reverie was interrupted by Paul VI.

"Shalom," said His Holiness, and Dunin realized he wasn't going to have to kiss that ring after all. Then the Pope motioned to his aide, Cardinal Vincenzi, who brought forward a delicate silver tray on which were two fragile glasses of the finest crystal and a bottle of slivovitz.

The cardinal poured them each a drink, and the Pope raised his glass in a toast.

"L'chayim," said the Bishop of Rome.

This was going to be a highly unusual meeting.

After a little polite conversation, Dunin found himself seated in front of the gilt desk where the Pope was carefully placing his signature on a document. It was a statement as revolutionary as if the Catholic Church had declared it was licensing the Monastery of St. Benedict to manufacture con-traceptives. For centuries, it had been withheld. Now, it was being signed with a flourish under the eyes of the ambassador from Israel.

"This papal encyclical," Paul VI said to Dunin as he finished, "is being sent to every diocese of the Catholic Church. It is the first official pronouncement from the Holy See that declares categorically that the Hebrews did not kill

Jesus Christ. The Romans did. The evidence, we have decided, is irrefutable.''

"Thank you, Your Holiness," said Dunin. "You don't mind my saying the jury has been out an awfully long time?''

"You wouldn't have wanted us to jump to conclusions?''

"No, no, of course not," Ambassador Dunin said quickly. "You had to consider it from every angle. One hasty mistake, some innocent Roman centurion might still be in jail. I understand." The talk was back to normal diplomatic insincerities, and the ambassador felt on firmer ground. "Now, Your Holiness, is there anything my grateful country can do for you?''

"I thought you'd never ask," said Paul VI, shepherd of God, Keeper of the Flame, and sufferer from arthritis. "Last winter, during the boycott, my bedchamber was colder than a witch's elbow"—he used the papal euphemism—"and I understand we are in for another long, damp chill. My arthritis is killing me. My doctor isn't helping much, and it wouldn't look right if I went to the Christian Scientists. I've tried praying, but it still hurts. If our good friends in Israel could assure the Holy See of an adequate supply of heating oil at a fair price—''

Jesus Christ, thought Dunin before he remembered where he was, Golda must have been telling the truth. The Vatican's intelligence is the best in the world.

He promised to see what he could do.

As he left St. Peter's, Ambassador Dunin decided he could now afford to take a taxi back to the Israeli embassy.

"Drive by the Colosseum," he instructed the driver, "I have a feeling the Romans are going to start throwing Christians to the lions again.''

It was like old times. The black Lincoln Continental slid up to the portico of the White House, the one in Washington that is only a little less splendid than Schoenbaum's in Savyon, and out of it stepped the short, well-fed middle-aged former bon vivant with the dark, curly hair and the accent that hadn't been heard in these parts since the Hessians had that wild party across the Delaware.

Henry Kissinger was back. Nothing had changed, although the German accent had gotten a bit thicker during his retirement.

He was greeted in the Oval Office by President Carter and Secretary of State Cyrus Vance, the man whose appointment to Kissinger's former job Henry had hailed as "Brilliant! A perfect choice! As long as it couldn't be me!" And he had promised Vance to make himself available at any time his country needed him. It was presumed the country he was referring to was the United States.

After the usual jovial amenities and search for hidden microphones, the three men seated themselves, and Jimmy Carter got down to business. He was, after all, a trained engineer as well as a politician; to him graphs and computers were tools, not mysteries, and he got right to the heart of the matter.

"Gentlemen, Ah have just received a repo't from a group of ouah specialists who have arrived at the oilfields near Riyadh at the request of King Khalid."

"An old friend," said Henry. It was a phrase he could repeat, and did, at the mention of almost any name from Leonid Brezhnev to Jill St. John. He had known Khalid before the monarch had assumed the throne and before Kissinger had given up bachelorhood. In the interest of international harmony Kissinger had spent a lively evening with Khalid in the luxurious confines of his seraglio, which at the time numbered only twenty houris, who apparently made up in enthusiasm what they lacked in numbers, for it was noted the next morning that Henry's hair had acquired considerably more curl.

It was then that he made the remark for which he was to become famous. "My country," said Kissinger, "may she always be in the right. But my country, right or wrong!" And he had bravely returned to the seraglio on another dangerous shuttle for the United States.

Thus, he had inside knowledge of the situation in Saudi Arabia, perhaps a little farther inside than Khalid was able to manage, since even then he was quite old.

"Ouah specialists repo't," said President Carter, "that oil flow is slowin' down at such a rate that within two months the Saudi Arabian fields will be producin' no oil at all. They'll be drier than a witch's elbow"—he used the presidential euphemism—"and that po' country may be forced to the extraordinary expedient of *importin'* oil for their use."

"What would Saudi Arabia need oil for?" Henry wanted to know.

"The king," the secretary of state reminded him, "has eight Cadillacs and a harem."

"Oh, yes," Kissinger recalled, "they both use a tremendous amount. It's the dry climate," he explained.

"The problem is mo' serious than just lubrication." The President seemed genuinely worried. "The oil seems to be flowin' deeper into the groun'. And ouah satellite photographs indicate the Pinskah Street oilfiel' in Israel is almost explodin' with new gushers caused by some undergroun' pressure in the Schoenbaum. We're not even sure what a Schoenbaum is; it's some new code word we've intercepted while buggin' Golda's hot line."

Kissinger hadn't even heard the last sentence. "Israel!" he shouted, leaping to his feet and starting to pace. "I don't want to go back! They'll mug me at Ben-Gurion Airport!"

"You promised," Vance reminded him. "You gave your word, if your country ever needed you—"

"Anyplace but Israel! It's impossible to get a decent quiche lorraine there! The water is terrible, there's always a chumsin, and Golda doesn't like me!"

"Ah thought you-all got along so well with the ol' girl? What happened?" the President wanted to know.

"She hates me because she doesn't speak English with an accent, and I do. 'After thirty years in a country,' she told me, 'even a German should be able to talk so every word doesn't sound like "Volkswagen,"' She thinks I'm putting it on."

"Ah doan think you-all are puttin' it on," said the President. "Soun's like nacherel talk to *me*."

"We have to regain Israel's confidence," Secretary Vance insisted. "They don't think we are really their friend."

"Why not? Before the election, didn't you people promise to give them four billion dollars' worth of arms?"

"Israel doesn't count what you say *befo'* an election," said the President sadly. "It's the mornin' after they're interested in. They are very unfair."

"We have to show them we are their friends," continued Vance. "They seem to be upset that the President is from the South and I'm from the North. They would prefer to talk to somebody from the East, hopefully the East Side, like Bella Abzug. But we can't appoint her. Ms. Abzug's idea of diplomacy is to holler on everybody; she'd be like another Israeli."

Kissinger nodded understandingly. "You wouldn't be able to tell her from Yigael Allon," he agreed, "except for the hat."

"It's a delicate situation," the new secretary of state continued. "It looks like Israel is going to wind up with all the oil in the Persian Gulf. We want to be able to buy it at the best possible price. We have to make them understand that we respect their country, we honor their country, we are absolutely without prejudice against their country, and then maybe we can jew them down." He looked up, startled at his own words. "Oops," said the secretary of state. "Bad choice of verb. But you get the idea."

"Volkswagen," said Henry, or at least it sounded like it. What he actually was saying was: "Why do you want *me?*"

"Beco'se," said President Carter, "you-all have the raht mixture of arrogance, intelligence, an' snobbishness they-all respec'."

"Snobbish?" exclaimed Kissinger. "*Moi?*"

It was an old joke, and it went over like one.

"And in addition," Secretary Vance explained, "you are Jewish."

"My God," said Henry suddenly, "that's right! I'd forgotten."

"Agreed, then," the President said, pressing the advantage. "You-all will accep' the delicate mission of persuadin' Mrs. Meir to sell all her oil at a faih price to us goood ol' boys on Pennsylvania Avenya?"

"I'm Jewish," Kissinger repeated, still trying to get used to the idea. It was difficult. He was now married to a shiksa and was fourteen private clubs removed from his bar mitzvah.

"Ah need yo' answer right now," said the President. "Time is a-wastin'."

"I'll do it," Kissinger said, "for God, for country, and for my beloved parents, who were really Unitarians."

The President and the secretary of state relaxed, with a sigh of relief. Good old Henry. He was off on his final and most difficult mission. Difficult, because this time it was Israel that held all the aces. The Israelis had been impossible when all they held was a pinochle deck with chicken fat stains on the deuces.

The distinguished group shook hands, had a round of diplomatic scotch to seal the occasion, called in the White House photographer to take a Polaroid, since Henry was leaving on Air Force One in half an hour, and the President and the secretary of state ushered Special Envoy Kissinger to the door of the Oval Office.

"God speed," said the secretary of state, a man with an overdeveloped sense of history.

"Y'all flah straight to Tel Ayviv now," the President commanded. "Doan' stop off an' kiss any Ayrabs on the way."

"Volkswagen," agreed Henry Kissinger.

At the same time that Air Force One was preparing for

takeoff for Tel Aviv with Special Envoy Kissinger, burning thirty barrels per minute of Persian Gulf oil while stacked up on the runway, a huge British Airways 747 was approaching Kennedy Airport in New York City. An extraordinary night session of the United Nations General Assembly had been convened for that very evening, at the request of the Arab League. Seated in the luxurious first class section of the double-decked transport was Yasir Arafat, dressed in the usual grimy fatigues and kaffiyeh which had become his trademark, earphones firmly in place as he watched the movie screen. *A Star Is Born* was tonight's picture. Since La Streisand's films are banned in Arab countries, this was Arafat's first opportunity to see her and figure out which one of them had stolen the other's nose.

However, the movie was only a minor feature of his journey; as head of the Palestine Liberation Organization he was about to make another dramatic appeal for help from the UN. Given the success of his previous appearance, when he had received a standing ovation from the General Assembly, he felt this encore could result only in a world boycott of Jewish oil until the Israeli government agreed to return to Arab control all the captured land plus the Pinsker Street Gusher. The old man who had started it all by digging a well for water in traditional Palestinian territory was to be branded a war criminal for allowing it to siphon off millions of barrels of oil legally belonging to the Arab world.

Arafat was already counting the probable vote in his head: as always, 110 to 0 against Israel, 14 abstentions, 11 calling in sick, and 9 stuck in traffic without gas. Even a revolutionary could feel comforted by something this traditional, which never varied and which gave one a sense of stability in an otherwise rootless world. A vote in the UN was as good as a visit to the family during Ramadan, he thought.

Perhaps he would not have been so sanguine had he been able to hear the chattering over the radio in the 747's huge pilot compartment. An Air France 727 had been hijacked after leaving Athens by three passengers, one man and two women, carrying hand grenades. They were demanding the release of three hundred PLO terrorists in Israeli hands. So far, comfortingly familiar. But wait. The control tower at Benghazi, Libya, was refusing them permission to land. A first. Premier Idi Amin Dada had come on the radio in person to warn them that if they landed in Uganda, he would have them arrested, bound hand and foot, and forced to watch all nineteen motion pictures that had been made about the Entebbe raid before executing them personally with a baseball bat. And while he was on the air, he wanted to say hello to Nadya Haffaz, wherever she was.

The terrorists then asked permission from their good friends and political brothers to land in Moscow. Word came back immediately that while World Communism was solidly behind all freedom-loving enemies of the imperialistic nation of Israel, an epidemic of swine flu had broken out at Moscow Airport and there was no one in the control tower, since they had run out of Kleenex.

A final desperate plea to Comrade Fidel Castro in Havana brought a prompt reply, in hasty Spanish: El fornicato yourselves.

The winds of change were blowing.

When Yasir Arafat strode to the dais at the UN General Assembly late that night, he could feel the tension in the air. His compatriots on the Arab League delegation had told him, somberly, that the government of Mexico, which had always in the past voted solidly against Israel, had informed them that the peso had sunk so low the Mexican delegation was hitchhiking to New York. They probably would not arrive in time to be counted, unless they could steal a bus. The others felt this was a subterfuge; Mexico, Paraguay, Colombia, which had so much in common with their Arab brothers, although no one had figured out what it was, were all playing for time. In true international fashion, they wanted to wait before deciding which horse to back until they knew who had fixed the race. It could be that the pendulum of oil diplomacy had swung in favor of Israel. But, and there was always the nagging but, suppose the Schoenbaum leaked? Stranger things had happened.

Arafat took his place at the podium. He reached into his pocket for his prepared speech and was comforted to feel that his pistol was still in place. It always made him feel more confident of his rhetoric. He cleared his throat and started to address the Assembly. It was one of his better efforts, impassioned, unreasoned, inflamed. In a last-minute note penciled in the margin, he added a plea for the poor hijackers in the Air France 727, at that moment circling over Monte Carlo, appealing to Princess Grace as their last hope. One heartless newsman had suggested they ask the princess to put ten thousand francs in their name on a hard eight at the casino; if they crapped out, they could always ditch into the Mediterranean.

Arafat felt this attitude was hardly comforting. What was needed, he shouted, was the complete elimination of the state of Israel. Certainly no one in this august body would be swayed by crass considerations of economic need for energy! Whatever the future held, even if the stories about the Pinsker Street Gusher should prove true, every nation represented here could easily switch over to solar power within eighty-four years, a mere flyspeck on the face of time as reckoned by the Prophet Mohammed, and this Zionist economic tyranny would be ended almost before it began!

He finished and waited for the applause. There was none. He looked over at the Israeli delegation, which had not walked out this time, and saw that the Israeli ambassador was munching on a bunch of dates that had just been handed him by the ambassador from Kuwait. It did not look promising. In stony silence, Arafat left the podium and went to take his seat. An attendant informed him, apologetically, that they had been unable to figure out what country the PLO represented; therefore, under UN regulations he would have to get a ticket and take his place in the visitors' gallery. He assured Arafat he would get a good view from there, and it also had a Coca-Cola machine.

A vote was immediately taken on a resolution from the government of Abu Dhabi. It was to the effect that Yasir Arafat should be directed to get a shave. And have his fatigues dry cleaned and pressed. It passed 144 to 0 with no abstentions, a landmark.

Arafat, outraged, tried to fight his way back to the podium, shouting hoarsely that it was a Zionist plot. As he was climbing up on the stage, a report was issued over the loudspeakers that President Carter had announced Henry Kissinger's departure for Tel Aviv, followed by an Associated Press bulletin reporting that the wife of the president of Gulf Oil had applied for membership in Hadassah.

There could no longer be any doubt. The Pinsker Street Gusher was accepted as reality. As Arafat reached the microphones and started to speak, the entire General Assembly rose to its feet as a man and walked out. Outraged, the leader of the PLO pulled out his revolver and sent a bullet crashing through the glass window of the broadcasting booth, where Eric Sevareid was calling him a shlimazl. The bullet missed, and Sevareid calmly continued, reporting that the Security Council had just passed a resolution condemning Mohammed as a racist.

The 727 finally received permission to land in Warsaw. The local Polish joke was that the control tower thought it was a turkey.

11 Yenta Disease in the White House

THE PINSKER Street Oil Conglomerate had shiny new offices on the twelfth floor of Kikar Malchei, some of them taken over from the water department. From the windows of the palatial surroundings, Manager Chaim-Harold Barak had a lovely view of the horizon and the black smudges that were the gushers on Pinsker Street, hurling Israel's wealth into the sky before pumping it safely into the huge tanks and pipelines that fed the ships that jammed Israel's harbors from Haifa to Eilat. When he pressed a button on his desk, Chaim also had a lovely view of his redheaded secretary's sensational bosoms as she and they bounced in to take dictation. The secretary's name was Rivka; her left one Chaim had named Zivka and the right one Mivka. He hadn't told Rivka, of course. The time didn't seem as ripe as she was yet. After all, Chaim was still a happily married man, Sonya kept telling him. Every night he went home to the Savyon White House, where Schoenbaum had given the couple the Lincoln bedroom as their very own, and after dinner with his father-in-law and a look at the dirty movies on Damascus television, Chaim and Sonya would retire, and Chaim would chase Sonya around Abraham Lincoln's four-poster until she figured he was too tired.

But she was wrong. All the time that Chaim was chasing Sonya, in front of his eyes he was seeing Rivka and Zivka and Mivka, and by the time he caught Sonya, who also turned him on mightily, he had his second wind and she had her first migraine.

"Chaim, stop!" she protested one night when he was trying to work his will on her. "I have a terrible headache."

"What do you mean, stop? I'm your husband; love, honor, and obey, you heard the rabbi."

"I didn't hear him say 'doggie fashion,'" Sonya insisted.

"He said it in Hebrew, right after *Baruch atah adonoy*."

"I don't believe you."

"All right, he didn't say it, but we're married! What's so terrible?"

"I'm a woman; I'm a person; I have a right to my dignity."

"I thought *I* had a right to your dignity, too. You said all I had to do was marry you to get it."

"Look, Chaim, I am no prude. I am willing to perform my conjugal duties just as long as you promise me a maid, my masseuse, two trips a week to the Tel Aviv branch of Vidal Sassoon, and you get home from the office every day at five thirty. But where does it say conjugal duties include hanky-panky?"

"In the Bible. It says, quite clearly, hanky-panky began in Israel, at Sodom and Gomorrah. I am merely trying to continue an ancient Hebrew tradition. When I say, 'doggie fashion,' those are not my words, but God's."

"I wish I could see it as God's will."

"Make an effort," Chaim urged.

"No. These are no longer biblical times. Right now, in

Sodom, which is a nice little industrial town on the edge of the Dead Sea, they just formed a chapter of women's lib. There is also one in Gomorrah, a sleepy little suburb.''

"Turn over," said Chaim, who hadn't been paying much attention.

"You know what the slogan of women's lib in Sodom and Gomorrah is? 'Down with Up!' It's a new day. You'll have to face it, Chaim."

"How can I face it when you won't turn over?"

"Go to sleep. I told you I have a headache."

She closed her eyes, the matter settled. When women discovered a harmless ailment that could be neither detected nor cured, they were halfway to total victory over their husbands. If they did not approve of a timing, a position, a bit of adventure, instantly shooting pains in the temples. What husband could transport himself on waves of pleasure while his wife was moaning that her head was coming off? In such circumstances, the male discovered his potency lessening with every moan, until finally his performance had to be canceled because of migraine and his wife got a good night's rest.

Chaim-Harold groaned and tried to sleep. It was no use. After a while, he started counting, "Rivka, Mivka, Zivka."

It didn't work.

Schoenbaum, of course, knew nothing of the sexual desert in which his son-in-law was wandering. How could he understand that to Sonya the ultimate triumph of the liberated woman was the subjugation of the liberated male? It was her revenge on that nudnik from Eighth Street and his active leather belts. Schoenbaum had gotten his daughter Sonya married; that was as far as the Torah and Sophie's memory commanded him. What went on in the Lincoln bedroom was none of his business. It wasn't even Lincoln's.

Meanwhile, Schoenbaum was living a dream. His voice was reckoned with in the councils of government. Golda had sent out word: "Don't mix in with Schoenbaum; he still owns the property."

Nobody mixed in. He suggested in Cabinet meetings that now that oil contracts were rolling in in such quantities and at such terms as boggled the mind, it was time to reduce the price of natural gas and put bottled water in the water pipes, people should be able to drink. He insisted that the import duties on television sets and automobiles, which amounted to three hundred percent of their original cost, should be abolished, so you didn't have to be a millionaire to own a Zenith and a Chevrolet at the same time. The sales tax should be eliminated; it soaked the poor more than the rich; a child should be able to buy a penny candy without paying four agorot to the government.

Golda agreed. It was all done. And Jacob Schoenbaum became the first and only idol of that forgotten man, the Israeli taxpayer.

Thus it was that when Special Envoy Henry Kissinger arrived, Prime Minister Golda Meir invited him to a private lunch at her house on Hayarkon Street with herself and Schoenbaum, the Voice of the People. When Kissinger got out of his limousine, he was pleased to see the huge throng outside Golda's modest home, figuring that his public was awaiting him at last. He had never been very popular in Israel before. However, he was a little puzzled when he noticed that all those in the crowd were wearing long black coats, in the middle of a chumsin, topped by long black beards and black fur hats pulled down around their ears and over their payes, their braided sideburns.

They were chanting, "Schoenbaum! Schoenbaum!" and a

few of them had dropped to their knees on Golda's lawn. Puzzled, Kissinger managed to push his way into the house with the help of his Israeli army escort. Golda and Schoenbaum were awaiting his arrival with a pitcher of cold lemonade, which Kissinger discovered quite refreshing, in lieu of Dom Pérignon. Golda greeted him warmly, preferring to let bygones be bygones, and accepted with thanks the little jar of peanut butter he had brought from the President. It was the thought that mattered, she said. The Shah of Iran had sent diamonds.

Schoenbaum was waiting impatiently in the background. Golda placated him by introducing him to Kissinger with proper formality.

"Mr. Special Envoy," she said, "this is Minister of Consumer Affairs Jacob Schoenbaum, to whom our country is eternally grateful. He has made Pinsker Street a household word and has changed the entire international diplomatic climate for our nation."

"In Israel," Schoenbaum informed his visitor, poking him with a finger, "they call me sometimes the Jewish Kissinger."

Henry realized he was in the presence of a world-class personality equaling his own. He retreated slightly from the finger and turned to the Prime Minister, genuinely interested.

"Why are all those bearded men outside shouting Schoenbaum's name? And why are they wearing overcoats during a chumsin?" he wanted to know.

"Oh," said Golda. "They're nudniks from the Neturey Karta, the Hasidic sect that's given us so much trouble. They are the Orthodox of the Orthodox. They've never recognized the government of Israel because the Bible says the Jews will get back the Promised Land only when the Messiah returns. And if the Messiah had already returned, would Israel be having such trouble as we used to have? So they wouldn't use our money, they wouldn't serve in the army, and fortunately, they wouldn't even vote. Also, they wouldn't fly on El Al, because it is owned by a government that doesn't exist in their eyes. Would *you* fly in an airplane with a mythical pilot?''

"But they seem happy," Kissinger noted, peering out of the window at the throng. The black-overcoated group was singing.

"Of course they're happy," Schoenbaum said. "They're all meshugge! They think the Messiah has returned!"

"Really?" inquired Henry, interested now.

"Henry, get away from the window," interrupted Golda. "It's not you; it's Schoenbaum."

"Meshugge!" repeated Schoenbaum. He opened the window. "Go away!" he shouted. "Leave already! By me if I was the Messiah, I would be in Israel in all this heat? In the Catskills I'd be, like everybody else!"

They shouted his name again, over and over, and finally, slowly, happily, they marched away, to vote, to spend money, and to fly on El Al. And to take off those long black coats until it cooled off.

The fur hats they kept on, as a gesture of reverence to Schoenbaum, the Messiah.

Once they were gone, Kissinger got down to business. The magnetic personality that had charmed the world's leaders for almost a decade was turned on like a klieg light, but now he was facing Golda Meir and Jacob Schoenbaum, the equivalent, in the political sense, of the Los Angeles Rams' Fearsome Foursome.

"The United States of America," he informed them, "Israel's greatest ally, has decided to furnish your country with everything Yitzhak Rabin asked for on his last visit: four hundred tanks, two hundred F-15 jet fighters, and twenty-five percent of the royalties from *Fiddler on the Roof.*" His eyes twinkled at the typical Kissinger pleasantry, the little joke he always slipped into negotiations to make the other side laugh and forget they would eventually be called on to pay for the tanks and planes.

"And what are we supposed to give you in return for all this generosity?" Prime Minister Meir wanted to know, her eyes not twinkling.

"Give? Nothing. How can we put a price on a friend's survival? What are friends for?"

"Friends," said Mrs. Meir, "are for not telling us to back up when we have the Egyptian Third Army surrounded."

Kissinger laughed. "I'd forgotten all about that," he said. "But I assure you, I had very good reasons for asking your country to be magnanimous at that time."

"Name one," said Golda.

"Volkswagen," said Kissinger, "Volkswagen, Volkswagen, Volkswagen."

And he poured himself some ice-cold lemonade from the pitcher Golda had set out, mopping his brow. Things had been easier in Peking.

"What did he say?" Schoenbaum asked Mrs. Meir, puzzled.

"Sometimes Henry is difficult to understand. Also, sometimes when he says one thing, he means something entirely different," Golda told him. "I have this direct from Jill St. John."

"Seems to me," Schoenbaum said, "he wants something, only he's afraid to come right out." He turned to the special envoy. "It's cold already in Washington; the President is used to Georgia weather. How much oil is America trying to get from us?"

"Listen, Schoenbaum," Kissinger said, "I've heard about you so I won't beat around the bush. The United States is in trouble. The Alaska pipeline froze solid."

"A child would have known this," Schoenbaum chided him. "You want to build a pipeline, build it by Palm Springs."

"I'll remember that next time. So we need all the oil you can sell us. All we ask is a fair price."

"All right," said Golda, "this is our price: The next time

we're winning, the United States shouldn't tell us we have to lose."

There was a stunned silence.

"You'll take all the fun out of the Middle East," Henry complained.

"Also," said Schoenbaum, a tough negotiator in his own right, "Pinsker Street oil we only sell direct to the consumer; it shouldn't go to the oil companies to take a commission and raise up ten cents every gallon."

"That's Communism!" cried Kissinger. "The oil companies won't have enough money to bribe anybody!"

"That's what I used to tell them down by NYU," said Schoenbaum, happily, the dreams of youth about to be realized. If only Sophie were here! He pressed his advantage, poking Kissinger with an experienced index finger.

"Pinsker Street Conglomerate should have its own gas stations," Schoenbaum insisted, "its own pumps, its own oil, and from Texaco we want back our Mogen David star and they can keep Bob Hope."

Kissinger finished his lemonade and got to his feet. "I will report your terms to Washington," he said stiffly, "but I don't hold out much hope that a Democratic Congress will approve."

"Look who's coming up the walk!" exclaimed the prime minister. "Ronald Reagan!"

"Make some more lemonade," suggested Schoenbaum, the Messiah.

While Ronald Reagan was having a cooling drink at Golda Meir's, Chaim-Harold Barak was heating up at the door to the Lincoln bedroom in the Savyon White House. His new wife had locked it from the inside.

They had had a lover's quarrel. Sonya had complained that Chaim was spending too much time at the office, now that he had an office, and was not arriving home promptly at five thirty, a time she was certain the rabbi had mentioned in the ceremony. Chaim had replied that there was no point in arriving home at that hour, because at five thirty Sonya always insisted she had a headache and refused to enter the bedroom. Sonya said no liberated woman went to bed at five thirty. Chaim pointed out this was no ordinary bedroom, but the Lincoln bedroom, and he was certain that although Abraham Lincoln might have liberated Mrs. Lincoln along with the slaves, he probably still insisted on a regular five thirty matinee. Sonya hinted darkly that if this were true, she was certain Mrs. Lincoln had dressed up as John Wilkes Booth when they went to the theater that fateful night.

It was a test of wills, the liberated woman versus the medieval mensh, as she called Chaim-Harold, and since they were truly in love, it included constant vituperation, threats of divorce, and an enjoyable period of making up, although not at five thirty.

Today Chaim-Harold had decided to assert himself. Fortified by a double slivovitz martini at the Waldorf-Astoria bar which melted the olive, he had arrived at the White House precisely on schedule, fire in his eye as well as his throat. He had visions of discovering Sonya in the rose garden picking the fragrant flowers, sweeping her off her feet, carrying her manfully in his arms up the circular staircase, then throwing her into the huge four-poster and catching her on the first bounce, after which they would continue to bounce together. It was a romantic image worthy of Elizabeth Barrett Browning, but unfortunately, when he arrived at the White House, Sonya was under the dryer she had installed in the Oval Office. When Chaim-Harold attempted to pull her out, he knocked the dryer over, singeing her hair, his hands, and a copy of the Declaration of Independence which was lying, framed, on the presidential desk.

Sonya ran screaming up the circular stairway with Chaim-Harold in hot pursuit. Warren Gamaliel Harding, who had participated in similar scenes in the White House, although not with his legal wife, stared down at them reminiscently from his portrait on the wall. Chaim-Harold was not amused, especially when Sonya beat him into the bedroom by four-tenths of a second and slammed and locked the door in his face. She had broken Wilma Rudolph's record for the hundred-meter stairway.

Chaim-Harold pounded on the door and shouted, "Open up!"

"Stop shouting!" Sonya shouted. "I've got a headache!"

"So what else is new?" inquired Chaim, to whom this was beginning to sound like a broken record. "You don't have a headache; you've got Yenta Disease!"

The worst thing you can call an old Jewish woman is yenta, because a yenta is an old Jewish woman. To call a young Jewish woman by this name is an invitation to mayhem. Luckily, the door would not come unlocked, and Sonya was reduced to pounding futilely on her side as Chaim-Harold pounded on his.

"Yenta!" he shouted, having found the key to her anger.

"Momzer!" she shouted back. "Slimazl!" She was sobbing now, for she realized she had lost the serenity that is the sign of the liberated female and had not yet discovered Chaim-Harold's magic word.

"Open up," Chaim pleaded. "We'll go to bed. I'll teach you how to pronounce '*sh*limazl.'"

"Never!" she shouted. "Every day you're five minutes late; you're playing around with the girls in the office!"

"In five minutes? Now *I*'m insulted!"

"I want a divorce!"

"Open the door, I'll call my lawyer."

"Never! Go back to your girls at the office!"

"Nag, nag, nag!"

"Lie, lie, lie!"

Only two people who really loved each other could have continued such a banal conversation for half an hour, but Chaim and Sonya loved each other very much, so it went on for forty-five minutes. When there was nothing left to say, the door still remained locked.

Sonya was crying. Chaim-Harold was determined. If he were going to have to put up with this day after day, he would have to find some way to deserve it.

"All right," he shouted, hoarsely, "I'll go find a girl, just to make you jealous!"

"Go, with my blessing," Sonya shouted back. "Find some old yenta!"

"One was enough," shouted Chaim-Harold, the momzer, and their marriage hung by a thread.

It was the strangest emergency session the Israeli Cabinet had ever held. The ministers assembled in the conference room in the government building in Jerusalem while it was still being redecorated. Warm wood paneling was being installed on the walls, a gift from little, freezing Finland; on the floor, a luxurious Persian rug, another gift from the Shah. The severe wooden chairs had been replaced with Barcaloungers; press a button, and the rich leather upholstery vibrated your back, while the chair tilted to a reclining position—a thoughtful gift from Anwar el-Sadat.

The Prime Minister called the meeting to order over the sharp protests of Schoenbaum. This was all a trick, he complained. Luxury had no place in Israel. Make everybody comfortable, next thing you know, the Arabs will attack, the whole country will be at the beach. This could be the enemy's secret plan: Strike at the very roots of Israel's strength, the discomfort of daily living that hardened a populace to the point where a little war was sometimes a welcome diversion. He suggested that all the oil money that was now rolling in should be invested in fertilizer. It would stimulate the economy without lowering the discomfort.

He was voted down. Mrs. Meir then gave a full account of their meetings with Henry Kissinger and Ronald Reagan.

"I believe Mr. Reagan is already running for the next presidency," she reported, "maybe a little too hard. He claims he has recently converted to Judaism and last week had a bris performed at Mount Sinai Hospital, with only a local anesthetic. Of course, we have only his word; we didn't ask for proof."

"Fortunately," added Schoenbaum.

"However, he did serve a valuable purpose. When Reagan got to my house, Henry Kissinger left by the back door. I'm sure Henry will report to the United States government that they had better give us everything we want, or Israel may back Governor Reagan in 1980. And there goes New York State. I think we should keep them guessing. It's still too soon to announce our choice and give Mr. Reagan the contribution he is asking, for his campaign fund, even though he promised to offer up a brucha for us at a synagogue of our choice."

There was general agreement; United States politics was too volatile. An unknown peanut farmer had been elected the last time; in the next election, who knows, Reagan might be beaten in the primaries by a lady barber. Better for newly important Israel, power broker to the world, to sit back and wait, relaxed in its Barcalounger, secure, for the moment, in its newfound strength, while in a dozen countries around the globe, at this very minute desperate Cabinet meetings were being held, all on a similar theme: How could Israel be convinced the last twenty-five years were just a bad dream? For, now, how could a democratic government stay in office without the approval of the oil barons of Pinsker Street?

It was a moment to be savored. But not for long.

"Now we come face to face with a problem Israel has never had before," said the Prime Minister. "We have signed enough contracts for Pinsker Street oil to bring in ten times the amount of our annual budget. Gentlemen, this is a crisis. Stop vibrating and pay attention."

They sat up now, realizing this was a moment in history never envisioned by the Prophets. They had warned against pestilence, pogroms, poverty, but not one Hebrew visionary had ever predicted prosperity. Shlimazls! Schoenbaum thought. They should turn in their beards!

"The money is becoming an embarrassment," Mrs. Meir told the Cabinet. "We have to put our new funds back into circulation, or we may destroy the economic stability of the world. Gentlemen, we must think: How can Israel spend twelve billion dollars in a hurry?"

Consternation. Until this moment no one had realized the immensity of the Pinsker Street Gusher and the Schoenbaum beneath it. And no Israeli Cabinet had ever faced the unheard-of problem of spending too much money.

Schoenbaum immediately shot to his feet. "Take down the taxes!" he hollered.

No one heard him.

The minister of the treasury cleared his throat. "I would suggest," he said, "that we should make a small move first. We must learn to walk before we can run. The first thing we should do is increase the salary of Cabinet ministers by two hundred fifty thousand dollars a year."

"Each?" inquired the Prime Minister doubtfully.

"Think big," encouraged the treasury minister. At the moment he was thinking of Nadya Haffaz. He might be able to afford to take her off the market. "You want Israel to look like a piker?"

"All in favor?" asked Golda Meir.

"Take down the taxes!" shouted Schoenbaum.

Again, no one heard him. The motion passed, twenty to one. It didn't matter that the one might be the Messiah.

The minister of the interior now had a suggestion. "Madame Prime Minister," he said, "have you noticed lately how Indira Gandhi dresses, even now when she's not prime minister? Class. Gold stripes in the blouses. Jewels in the hair. Necklaces, rings. And India is a poor country. Why should the Prime Minister of Israel walk around in an old shmatta of a dress, so big on her it makes her look like my bubba? The shoes are like herring boxes; the stockings are from cotton; the hair is falling down, could use a rinse, a tint, a wave. The whole country is swimming in oil, the Prime Minister has to look like she's on welfare?''

"It's better the dress is too big," Golda protested. "Have you ever seen my figure in a dress that fits?''

"Think big," said the minister of the treasury. "The figure is no good, change the figure! This is the new Israel! There are doctors, plastic surgeons; there are experts; there is the Golden Door. Take off something here, squirt in some silicone there, boom, Jacqueline Onassis!''

"Take down the taxes!" shouted Schoenbaum.

"You think it would work?" asked Golda musingly, thinking of the silicone, not the taxes.

"Of course!" It was the minister of defense. "France wants to send us more Mystères. First we'll ask they should fly in Yves St. Laurent; he personally will design for you a dress. Then you go take a nice vacation at the Golden Door until you fit it.''

"I don't think I should take that much time from the job," protested Golda, already halfway there. "It could be months.''

"So you'll fly home once a week," said the air force minister. "We'll buy for you a Lear Jet. Air Force Aleph, we'll call it, our own Air Force One. Remember, it's for Israel, how else can we get rid of so much money?''

"Take down the taxes!" hollered Schoenbaum.

"Yves St. Laurent," mused Golda. "You think he's the best?''

"So we'll also get Cardin, we'll get even Ted Lapidus, France needs two million barrels of oil; it'll come out absolutely even." The treasury minister had the figures down on paper already.

Golda was beginning to smile to herself. She remembered how it had been, when she was younger, when she had been in love. She remembered well the young Goldie Myerson, and while money could not bring back her youth, perhaps it could bring back her memories. What price could be put on them?

"What about England?" she said. "They're in such trouble; we should do something right away to help."

"You had something in mind?" It was Abba Eban, whose special province had been the British Empire ever since someone told him he sounded like Winston Churchill.

"Yes," Golda mused. "A St. Laurent dress, a Vidal Sassoon hairdo, maybe a Cardin scarf over the hair, what would look better with it than perhaps a small Rolls-Royce convertible? Not immediately, of course. Next year in Jerusalem."

The idea was approved by acclamation, except for one apoplectic messianic voice. Golda heard it at last. The Prime Minister turned to her Cabinet.

"All of our new wealth," she reminded them, "we owe to one member of this group, Jacob Schoenbaum of Pinsker Street. After we raise our salaries and buy the dress, I suggest we establish the Schoenbaum Rebate, returning to the taxpayers every agora they have paid this government in income tax in the last five years!"

Schoenbaum stopped hollering. Suddenly something in the back of his mind was sounding a warning. Too much tax relief was worse than too little. With nothing to complain about and no City Hall to fight, the Israeli élan might vanish completely. The taxpayers would grow flabby. The spirit of anger on which the country existed, the defiance of authority that had given the assistant water commissioner constant gas pains, the ability to live on the edge of a precipice, which had sustained the little country through four wars and several treaties of friendship— "Whom the gods want to punish, they give America for an ally," Ephraim Kishon had written—all these would be dulled by a period of taxless ease. It was not the first time the people of Israel had faced the awesome quicksands of a life of pleasure and succumbed. Sodom and Gomorrah. The pillar of salt.

"Thou shalt have no other God before me," Jehovah had

thundered at Moses, and the tribes had wandered for seven years in the wilderness. Now Golda was bowing down at the shrine of St. Laurent; instead of the golden calf, the Golden Door. Schoenbaum could feel the clouds of wrath gathering in the distance.

He voted loudly against the motion to buy the dress and return all taxes. No one else in that room on that fateful afternoon understood what was really happening. When the voice vote was called for, the Cabinet shouted fifteen ayes, and there were two nays, including Schoenbaum's, when only sixteen ministers were in the room.

Schoenbaum alone suspected where that second angry Voice was coming from.

Chaim Barak drove his four-door Mercedes down a Dizengoff Street ablaze with lights and theater marquees, a big cigar in his mouth, and Rivka, Zivka, and Mivka beside him in the front seat. This was it. D-Night. He was about to take his revenge on Sonya for refusing him four times running and twice walking. It would make her realize that her foolish insistence on Jewish Princesshood was endangering their marriage. He was doing it for her. It would only make Sonya love him more, he assured himself. He had called her at the Savyon White House and told her he was working late at the office, counting money. The story was plausible since that was a prime occupation of most of the country following the massive tax rebate. Prosperity was busting out all over, and so were Zivka and Mivka. Rivka, in honor of the occasion, was wearing her tightest dress with the deepest cleavage. The manager of the Pinsker Street Oil Conglomerate was no mean catch; she had wheeled up the heavy artillery.

The street was jammed with traffic; everyone, it seems, was driving either a Mercedes, a Cadillac, or a Ferrari. The *Folies Bergères* was opening, and there would have been a procession of chauffeur-driven limousines in front of the theater, but there weren't any chauffeurs in Israel anymore. They were now driving their own Mercedes.

Chaim and Rivka had had an intimate little dinner in a discreet, private booth at Maxim's. The famous French landmark had wisely moved from Paris to Yirmiyahu Street, Tel Aviv's Restaurant Row, where the Plintzi serves twenty-six types of sweet and salted blintzes and the Peer Oriental Steak House & Milk Bar daringly flaunts all the dietary laws. In this heady atmosphere, French gastronomy had been forced to extend itself: Maxim's famed crepes suzettes were now served in flaming shmaltz.

Maxim's champagne, however, was still French, and still effective. Rivka was resting her head on Chaim's shoulder, and her hand on his knee. Chaim was resting his hand on Zivka and Mivka, alternately, since simultaneously was impossible. He was encouraged when Rivka's only protest was a mild hiccup. They were heading for an elegant bagnio on Shaul Hamelekh Boulevard, with water beds and closed-circuit television, which had a hidden camera trained on the women's mikvah at the Waldorf-Astoria. It was the height of any Jewish boy's erotic fancy to see someone else's wife without her sheitel, the ritual wig Orthodox women always wear, except in the religious bath. Chaim was counting on the entire ambience to turn Rivka on, so they could raise whitecaps in the water bed.

Half an hour later, after another bottle of champagne in the privacy of their romantic room, Chaim was holding Rivka, Zivka, and Mivka in his arms and trying to get them down on the bed.

"Stop!" said Rivka.

It was an effort, but Chaim stopped. Sonya had gotten him into the habit.

"Rivkele," he whispered, "what's wrong? You don't love me?"

"Love, of course. But not *this*. At least, not until the divorce is final."

"What divorce?"

"Yours. From Sonya."

"Why should I divorce Sonya?"

"Because I'm a person, not a thing."

"Of course, you're a person; you've also got a beautiful thing."

"Don't be vulgar. And turn off that awful television, I just saw my mother without her sheitel."

Chaim hastily switched off the television set. What rotten luck. Already Rivka was putting her seamless pantyhose back on.

"I'm sorry," Chaim said, "but why did you come here with me if you want marriage first?"

"The champagne"—Rivka hiccuped—"also I thought this would bring things to a head; you would be forced to make a decision between two human beings, not two sex objects."

"Sounds like a slogan from women's lib."

"It is."

"Down with Up," said Chaim sadly.

"Exactly. Now take me home. I live halfway between Sodom and Gomorrah."

"If only we'd met four thousand years ago." He sighed.

Chaim drove her home all the way to the Dead Sea, without speaking a word, past the mountain peak that is, according to tradition, the pillar of salt that was Lot's wife after she made the mistake of looking back. Chaim carefully avoided looking back himself; he was afraid he would see Rivka's mother running after them, without her sheitel.

While Israel was being demoralized by prosperity, the counterattack was launched. It was so carefully planned that no one recognized the danger at the time. No one except Jacob Schoenbaum.

On the surface, things had never been better. For the first time, the streets in Tel Aviv were actually clean, the buildings

painted, the taxi drivers polite. The Israeli pound became the
world's most stable currency. Money was withdrawn from
Swiss banks to be deposited in the Bank Hapoalim in
Jerusalem. Speculators drove the price of the West German
Deutsche mark so low, most Germans felt it had hardly been
worthwhile to lose the war.

Only Schoenbaum was farsighted enough to see the hidden
peril. Jewish guilt was disappearing. Every Jew knows in his
heart that he is not supposed to enjoy himself. If a Jew enjoys
himself, he must be disobeying one of the Commandments;
otherwise, why would he be happy? Therefore, he must feel
guilty. God will punish him, to balance things out. If it wasn't
this way on earth, what would be the point of heaven? Chaim,
for instance, at the crucial moment when Rivka revealed
Mivka and Zivka to him and he took the three of them in his
arms, kept reminding himself, "I'm not enjoying! I'm not
enjoying! Honest, God. It only looks that way, believe me."
But God was not fooled. Chaim was naked; an idiot could have
seen that he was affected pleasantly by Rivka, Mivka, and
Zivka, so God balanced things out by putting Rivka's mother
in front of the television camera without her sheitel. Justice
was done.

However, not feeling guilty began to become very popular
in Israel, in spite of the Lord's efforts. The Jewish work ethic
started to disappear. To Schoenbaum, any Jewish man who
didn't work at least eight hours a day, except Saturdays, was a
bum. Now there was a nation of bums, supported by the government and the Pinsker Street Gusher. Since work was at a
minimum, Jewish men had more time to spend with Jewish
women. They weren't happy about it. It turned out that most
Jewish women had the same kind of work ethic in bed as
Sonya, Rivka, Zivka, and Mivka. The men were restless. The
devil always finds work for idle hands. Something had to be
done.

Schoenbaum brought the matter up before the next meeting
of the Cabinet in Jerusalem and was surprised to find that the

Prime Minister was in complete agreement. She was wearing a Cardin pants suit, a St. Laurent scarf, and a bouffant hairdo, with tiny curls bunched about her forehead, and still looked like somebody's bubba. But her Rolls-Royce was standing by at the King David Hotel to rush her to the airport, where her Lear Jet was fueled for the first leg of the journey to the Golden Door. In a few weeks everything would fit. Or her money back. How could her country lose?

"Of course," Golda told her ministers, "we must protect the women of Israel, who have a tradition to uphold. But I was young once"—she paused and smiled, reminiscently; it didn't seem so long ago, now that her ears had been pierced and little diamonds twinkled in them again—"and I know how impatient men can be. Our country is prosperous, but not happy. It so happens we have just received a cable that may offer a solution." She turned to the foreign minister, Eban, who had abandoned his stiff formality for blue jeans and a sweat shirt chauvinistically stenciled "Up with Down! *Chacun à son goût!*"

"Abba," Mrs. Meir ordered, "read the cable."

Foreign Minister Eban got to his feet and adjusted his glasses. He was not too comfortable in his mod dress but felt it necessary to show himself aware of the changes that were taking place; as one of the last remaining old guard, he had to identify with the new guard. The sweat shirt had pained him, so he had added the line in French to give it class. Public opinion polls showed his popularity rising. If he kept moving in the right direction, and Golda decided not to come back from the Golden Door, and the two shruggers were too busy with Nadya Haffaz, he might yet be the People's Choice. So he wore the sweat shirt.

"TO THE GOVERNMENT OF ISRAEL, SALAAM ALEIKUM," he read. "I, SHEIKH BIN SAID, SULTAN AND MONARCH OF OMAN, HAVE BEEN DISTRESSED BY THE RECENT FAILURE OF OUR ONCE-OVERFLOWING OIL FIELDS TO SUPPLY EVEN OUR BASIC NEEDS. WITHOUT OIL, OURS IS A LAND RICH ONLY IN THE

BEAUTY OF OUR WOMEN. IN EXCHANGE FOR A TWO-MONTH
SUPPLY OF THE BEST PENNSYLVANIA GRADE CRUDE, I OFFER
YOUR GREAT NATION MY MOST PRECIOUS POSSESSION, THE
TWENTY HIGHLY TALENTED HOURIS OF THE ROYAL SERAG-
LIO.''

There was a startled gasp from the assembled ministers as
his meaning sank in. The royal harem was negotiable! Certainly Israel could not accept such a ridiculous and immoral
offer. Schoenbaum was the first to leap to his feet. This might
be a fatal blow to family life; Israeli women would certainly
throw out of office any government sanctioning such an insane
negotiation!

"Not so fast," said the minister of defense, who had lately
been tiring of Nadya Haffaz's charms. "Maybe it's what our
women want. It would take the pressure off, at least they
would know where their husbands are, and they wouldn't be
forced to do something no Nice Jewish Girl should be forced to
do, especially on Shabbas. Arab women rest Fridays, Jewish
women Saturdays; it would spread things out."

"Believe me," said the minister of health, "the sale of
aspirin would drop in half; headaches might disappear."

"We're only talking one little harem," the treasury minister
reminded them. "Who could it hurt? And poor Oman is in
trouble; what else do they have to trade, camels?"

"It's a trick!" Schoenbaum shouted. "Wait, you'll see!
Remember, Schoenbaum said it!"

"Nonsense," said the quiet voice of Golda Meir. They all
turned. She was the only woman present; her opinion would
carry the most weight. "I don't think we can afford to pass this
opportunity by. One harem, these few women, how can they
harm Israel? A country that has absorbed three million immigrants is going to be disturbed by twenty girls with nice
tochis? They'll go on the stage; they'll go in a nightclub;
they'll give massages; maybe they'll get married—it's nothing.

"What is something is that this is the first little opening in the solid Arab front. One little country is breaking away from all the others, is willing to sit down and negotiate with us face to face. This is exactly what Israel has been demanding from the beginning. Straight out, Jew to Arab, man to man, like it should have been from the beginning. They want oil, our women need a rest; this could be the beginning of a small solution.

"The larger solution will be when the entire Arab League comes to us for oil, and we drive the only bargain that matters: peace. I don't care what we have to trade; it will be worth it. For you, for me, for our families, for our children, a secure future inside secure boundaries, the tanks and the guns on the scrap heap. For this, what difference does it make, a few Arab girls, a few Jewish men, a little incense, a few pillows on the floor, a little Benny Goodman on the radio?" Oy, thought Golda, I'm giving away my age.

"It's a trick!" warned Schoenbaum, but as usual no one was paying any attention.

Abba Eban was ordered to make the best possible deal with the sultan and bring it back for ratification. It was also suggested that he search for other soft spots in the Arab flanks. After all, there were twenty-one men in the Cabinet, and only twenty houris.

The matter settled, Prime Minister Meir left for the Golden Door. By the next Cabinet meeting she might be able to make the numbers come out even.

The first harem arrived at Ben-Gurion Airport by way of Cyprus, since there was as yet no direct air traffic between Israel and the Arab world. The twenty beautiful dark-eyed girls were frightened, but curious. For most of them, it was their first journey outside the seraglio since the sultan had either bought or been given them as gifts and had finished unwrapping. Of course, in this more modern age, even in the harem they had access to phonographs, radios, and magazines and were far from unworldly. In fact, they had been living a life devoted completely to the kind of sensuality only recently advocated in the West's various media and rarely achieved outside the center spreads of the magazines themselves. For more than a thousand years Arab girls had been acting out the kind of dreams even Hugh Hefner couldn't afford.

They were met at the plane by the immigration authorities and hurried off to the relocation centers maintained by the Israeli government to train new immigrants and place them in jobs. The girls proved to be a problem, just as the Arab League had intended. They had been chosen for the harem because they loved their work; the sultan, although he did his best for them, was after all only one man, although he had large appetites. Theirs were barely appeased. Now, in Israel, they were thrust suddenly into a civilization where their charms were move obvious by contrast. The sabra girls, strong, forthright, disdaining makeup, displaying muscles developed during hard work cleaning chicken coops in the kibbutzim or firing automatic weapons in the army and destined, as everyone knew, to turn into Jewish Princesses after marriage, were in another and minor league. It wasn't long before the relocation authorities, who were for the most part male, decided it was wrong to try to mold new immigrants to the Israeli image; it might do irreparable harm to their psyches. The girls were allowed to choose their own region to live in and the work for which they were best trained.

Shortly after this decision the first advertisements appeared in Israel's leading newspaper, *Ma'ariv,* in Hebrew: "!ecivreS llactuO harromoG & modoS !gninepO dnarG." There were several provocative pictures of the new immigrants in their working clothes and, underneath, a testimonial signed by the sultan: "!ffo tah ruoy kconk ot deetnarauG." The telephone number followed: 96.

What further followed was a large part of the male population in the Dead Sea area, which proved to be not so dead after all. Lot's wife would have been proud of her old hometown.

Israeli men found Arab ways to their liking. The girls didn't ask for the keys to the car, they didn't want to get married, they didn't complain if you came late from the office, and most of all, they never had headaches. Absolutely never, no matter how much dignity they were losing. The Promised Land was finally living up to its promise.

Of course, there was great discontent in parts of Israel which were too far from the Dead Sea for easy pilgrimages. It was considered only equitable to allow a few more of the harems to immigrate, since it was helping destroy the solidity of the Arab League. Soon the signs of Israel blazed with invitations: BEN YEHUDA STREET BOTTOMLESS! BIBLICAL WATER BEDS! HASIDIM WELCOME—WEAR YOUR OVERCOATS!

Chaim-Harold Barak-Bernstein grew to know the road to Gomorrah well, after that disappointing evening with Rivka, Zivka, and Mivka. He and Sonya were still not getting on, despite the efforts of a worried Jacob Schoenbaum to mediate their disputes. Even Henry Kissinger would have thrown in the towel.

Chaim decided that to continue to save their marriage, he would be forced once more to do something to bring Sonya to her senses, for her own good. He was one of the first to venture to try the magic telephone number in *Ma'ariv* and forgot to feel any Jewish guilt when a melodious voice informed him that he had a choice: Sodom and Gomorrah Outcall could supply a dancer to dance at his place, or he could come to the luxurious replica of the sultan's seraglio in Gomorrah, where he could select his dance partner in person. There was also curb service, if his time was limited and his car was large.

Chaim's Mercedes was zooming down Gomorrah's main street within two hours. In a vacant field adjoining the Chamber of Commerce, a huge tent had been pitched. A sign proclaimed, PILLAR OF SALT PLAYBOY CLUB. OUR BUNNIES HUG.

Incense wafted over the surrounding area. Camels wandered

about an enclosure complete with Bedouin tribesmen and their goats, somewhat nullifying the incense but lending an air of desert mystery to the setting. An Arab attendant in a creamy white burnoose took Chaim's Mercedes at the tent, remarking that his father had four automobiles exactly like it in the old country; he was only parking cars because he got paid in trade.

Inside, the luxury increased. Delicate tapestries, deep Persian rugs, golden oil lamps casting flickering shadows, silken curtains dividing individual boudoirs, strewn with soft pillows. Chaim was ushered in by a charming Arab girl who took his shoes, his jacket, and his American Express card. He was seated on the floor, reclining on a dozen satin pillows, as the new immigrants paraded for his inspection to the music of a flute and tambourine. The girls' faces were veiled, in the tradition of the Near East, but their undulating bodies were barely covered, just a tiny G-string that wouldn't have served Nadya Haffaz as an eye patch.

Chaim had a terrible time selecting his merchandise. He understood now how women could get more pleasure from window-shopping than from buying. One of the girls possessed close relatives of Zivka and Mivka, but the hurt was too recent, and Chaim finally picked a more delicate, but still shapely, former employee of the sultan of Oman, with the incredible name of Salome. Pleased, she gently ushered him into one of the curtained boudoirs and carefully removed his clothing. It was hardly necessary to remove her own.

"Wait a minute," said Chaim. "You sure you're not going to get a headache all of a sudden?"

Smiling, Salome shook her head. "I would get fired," she informed him. "It's against union regulations." And she started, carefully, to kiss him in several places he had never before considered kissable.

"How did a nice girl like you ever get into the harem business?" he wanted to know, sighing happily.

"All you Jewish men ask me that," she said, pausing in her work.

"Don't stop," said Chaim.

"I must stop if you want me to talk."

"Maybe you could use sign language?"

She laughed and stretched out beside him, using her hands for a kind of sign language Chaim had never studied, but every word was clear.

"If you want to know the truth," Salome said, "high school in Juwara was no big deal. I mean, the boys would take us over to Khaluf or Muscat on Saturday nights to watch them shear sheep, then maybe they'd butcher a goat and we'd have a cookout in the desert near Jabal Akhdar, but it always ended up with a roll in the sand, and that can be painful."

"I can see how it might be," Chaim agreed, intrigued by this look at a strange civilization and also by Salome's left hand, gentle as a butterfly. "Could you try a little higher?" he inquired tentatively.

"Your wish is my command," the beautiful dark-eyed Arab employee whispered. It occurred to Chaim he had never heard a Jewish Princess whisper anything like that. The closest Sonya had ever come had been one feverish night, when she had said, "Please, darling, go ahead, but don't ask me first!"

"You hated high school?" Chaim inquired, between sighs, hoping to prolong the conversation.

"Of course. I had a drip of a homeroom teacher, chased me all over the gym during recess. He wanted to marry me. You know what he had in the bank? I bet about two pieces of goat cheese and some stale olives."

"He doesn't sound like your kind. You want me to turn over?"

"It's what *you* want, not what *I* want."

"It's tough for me to get used to that idea," Chaim said apologetically. "You'll kind of have to lead, I'll follow."

"You poor shlimazl." Salome sighed. "It's difficult to believe Solomon went to the same shul as you."

She started leading. Chaim followed eagerly.

"You want to know what happened after high school?" Salome whispered as she nibbled on his ear.

"I hope you didn't go all the way through college? I don't think I could last until graduation."

"Don't worry. I dropped out of high school my freshman year. My mother flipped her wig, so I ran away to the Big Apple. Matrah. That's where the sultan lives. For a while things were tough. I baked pita, sold magazine subscriptions. *Literary Digest, Collier's*. In Matrah they haven't heard yet they're out of business."

"Keep leading," said Chaim, panting, "but don't gain on me too much. Tell me, how did you meet the sultan?"

"Oh, I didn't have to meet him. Every February they hold auditions."

"Auditions?"

"Of course. The sultan's harem is the big time. A little dancing, a little singing. A session in the back room with a talent scout. Don't call us, we'll call you. You know the routine."

"I've never auditioned for a harem," Chaim confessed. "Listen," he said, "you sure this won't give you a headache?"

"Don't be silly. This is the same routine I used for my audition. I knocked them dead."

"Next day on your dressing room they hung a star?"

"Exactly. I got the job. But the sultan is an old man; the harem has a lot of girls, turned out to be a big bore. I'd sit around most of the time, writing letters to my mother, to that nudnik in my homeroom, anybody. I wasn't learning anything. I was getting soft. My wind was going. All the men around were eunuchs. There was no incentive. I started getting homesick for a roll in the sand near Jabal Akhdar. So when they asked for volunteers to go to Israel, I was the first to hold up my hand."

"I'm glad you did," said Chaim, whose blood pressure had been steadily increasing under Salome's expert guidance.

"Now comes the big test," he said. "I'm going to ask you to do something no Jewish girl would ever do for me at a moment like this."

"What's that?" she inquired, a little fearful.

"Shut up," Harold informed her.

Sonya Barak-Bernstein hadn't seen her errant husband for three nights running when Chaim called and said he was coming home to the White House. She tried to sound cold and distant, but the moment Sonya hung up the tears of happiness came. She knew now she really and truly loved him. In a way, she could even understand him. Perhaps her insistence on the code of the Jewish Princess had been a mistake. Perhaps all that Chaim had been looking for was the Sonya of Christmas Past, who had been willing to give him the sort of gifts no Santa Claus could deliver.

Quickly, with growing excitement, she slipped into her sheerest nightgown, although it was early afternoon. She carefully applied her makeup and brushed her hair so it would hang loosely about her shoulders, the way she had worn it when they had first met. This whole incident would make a good opening for her novel, she decided. She hadn't learned to type, since she hadn't yet bought the typewriter, but she was thinking seriously of purchasing a tape recorder. It might be possible to live a scene and dictate it at the same time, if she had a finger free to press the microphone button.

Sonya found her pink silk robe and slipped it on, leaving it provocatively open in front. When she heard Chaim's footstep on the stairs leading to the Lincoln bedroom, she promised herself she wouldn't tell him her secret. Not yet. Not until afterward, in the huge four-poster, under the eyes of the portrait of the Great Emancipator, which, if he had been watching his bed closely, would probably be crossed by that time.

The door opened, and there he stood, Chaim-Harold Barak-Bernstein, looking a little tired, but happy.

"Chaim!" cried Sonya. She was about to run to him and throw her arms about him, but the last vestige of Jewish Princesshood prevented her from making the first move. It was up to him. All she did was open the robe wide. Chaim looked at his lovely wife, her charms visible beneath the sheer negligee, and made a mental computation. The sultanate of Oman by 3½ points. But it was close. It was an effort, but he would have to continue teaching his beautiful Sonya a lesson. He brushed her aside and started for the bathroom.

"Chaim!" She realized she had made a mistake and ran after him. "What's wrong? What did you come home for?"

Her husband found the bottle and put it in his pocket. He had been imagining this scene all day, and it was going according to plan. For her own good.

"My vitamins," he told his wife.

When William Congreve wrote, "Heaven has no rage like love to hatred turned, Nor hell a fury like a woman scorned," he must have had Sonya in mind. For as Chaim left, she thought she heard him mutter, "Yenta!" The chicken fat was in the fire.

Downstairs in the Oval Office, the Prime Minister was meeting with Schoenbaum. Mrs. Meir had just returned from the Golden Door in California, eighteen pounds lighter, her face lifted along with other areas, trying to get used to the idea of being an almost natural blonde. Now instead of looking like an old bubba, she looked like a young bubba. But still she was troubled. She had come to talk to Schoenbaum about what she had seen in the United States because he was the only one in the entire Cabinet who had warned against the path she was leading her country down.

"I've got to tell you, Schoenbaum," she said, "things are not good. The United Jewish Appeal, our friends of the UJA, couldn't believe it when I told them they didn't have to sell any more bonds, that Israel didn't need any more money. It was a body blow.''

''What's so terrible, they don't have to squeeze anybody to pledge?''

''You don't understand. Without bond drives, without having to call on the telephone, without having to ask Leonard Bernstein to give another concert for free, what do the women of the Hadassah have to do? No appeals, no donations, no charity affairs? It's a catastrophe. With so much time on their hands, they're staying home at night with their husbands, and neither one can stand it.''

''I can see they got here a problem,'' Schoenbaum agreed. ''For somebody else they couldn't raise money?''

''Who? Where else in the world are there any poor, starving Jewish people? Even in Russia, since the Brezhnev Triangle, things are better.''

Schoenbaum understood. The Brezhnev Triangle had been Abba Eban's greatest triumph. Russia, of course, had enough oil for its own uses, but every time a five-year plan took ten years Russia needed wheat from America. So the Brezhnev Triangle had been worked out: Israel sent oil to Russia, Russia sent it to the U.S. for wheat, the U.S. sent the wheat to Moscow, and Moscow sent Jewish emigrants to Israel.

Problems arose when stories of the new prosperity in Israel, plus the first rumors about the Pillar of Salt Playboy Club, reached beyond the Ural Mountains and created a certain amount of unrest among Russian men, most of whom had wives who looked like Golda Meir before the Golden Door. Thousands of Russian men converted to Judaism to be eligible to be exchanged for wheat. To stem the flow, Israel had to insist on Reaganism: No conversion would be deemed complete unless it included circumcision. Since Russian men were fearful that if there were any slight error, this procedure might make the Pillar of Salt Playboy Club academic, conversions had slowed down. Still, the rate was higher than the government of Israel would have preferred. But it certainly eliminated any thought of the UJA selling bonds for Russia.

Schoenbaum was about to suggest a solution when they heard the front door of the White House slam shut and a four-door Mercedes start up in the driveway. A moment later the door of the Oval Office flew open and Sonya ran in, her eyes flashing fire, her anger almost uncontrollable. She was still wearing her pink robe and her makeup; but the mascara was running, and she looked terrible.

"Papa!" she cried. "Chaim took his vitamins; he's moving out of the Lincoln bedroom; he called me a yenta!"

Suddenly, anger wasn't enough; she put her arms about her father, and the tears came, tears no liberated woman could admit to, but there they were. Schoenbaum's heart ached for her.

"What does this mean, moving out?" Schoenbaum wanted to know, all his fighting instincts aroused by his daughter's sorrow. "Lincoln never moved out; they had to shoot him!"

"I'm not going to take this anymore. I want a divorce," Sonya said and, seeing the Prime Minister, turned her anger and her tears on her. "It's all your fault! You wanted to make an opening in the solid Arab front, so what happens? Jerusalem is already one big massage parlor! In Bethlehem they have the Immaculate Conception Pussycat Outcall and Shish Kebab Service! Nice Jewish Girls are expected to compete with Arab belly dancers who couldn't get a headache at a gang bang, excuse the expression. Not one husband in Israel brought his wife breakfast in bed last week. They want us to bring it to *them*. You're destroying nagging, the basis of the Jewish family. Every time I tell Chaim he should pick up his own dirty socks he runs to Gomorrah. And I still love him! The momzer!"

She was fighting the tears again. Schoenbaum put his arms about his daughter.

"Shah," he said, "it's nothing. Boys will be boys. Soon he'll come back, you'll see. Too much belly dancing could kill him, vitamins or no vitamins. He'll come back, you'll holler on him, everything will be all right, you'll get a headache, Home Sweet Home!''

"I don't want him back," Sonya said. "He mustn't know I love him. I'll show him I'm truly liberated; I won't tell him about the baby.''

"What baby?" Golda, who had been lost in her own thoughts, brought herself out of her reverie. She had caught a glimpse of herself in the mirror and didn't like what she saw. The dress that fitted. The shoes with the slender high heels. The hair in gentle blond waves about the lifted face. The lack of wrinkles. This wasn't Golda Meir. More important, this wasn't Israel.

"What baby?" she repeated, the magic word having brought her back her maternal instinct.

"Mine," said Sonya. "I don't want Chaim to know I'm pregnant. It's my body; I'll get a little abortion. I hear it's no worse than a toothache. It will serve him right.''

"Wait!" said Schoenbaum, too outraged even to holler. "You could have my grandson, but you want instead a toothache?''

"Papa, I want your grandson, but what I don't want is a son from that belly-dance chaser!''

"Sonya, don't do this, all my life I waited!''

"I'm doing it! Papa, you of all people should understand what pride is. The marriage is finished. My mind is made up. No baby!''

"Sonya!''

"Papa, shhh, I got a headache.''

And Sonya ran upstairs to cry her heart out in the Lincoln bedroom, emancipated, but far from liberated.

Schoenbaum turned to the Prime Minister, his face ashen.

"Golda," he ordered, "you should take your bottle peroxide and go home.''

She nodded, acquiescing. Schoenbaum, as usual, was right.

Jacob Schoenbaum was not a drinking man. An occasional nip of slivovitz on the occasion of a wedding, a bar mitzvah, a bris, that was all. From that a man doesn't get drunk. But now his entire life had collapsed. His promise to Sophie was a hollow mockery. He had achieved the impossible by getting Sonya married. There the story was supposed to end. They should live happily ever after hollering on each other, just like Schoenbaum and Sophie. Divorce, in a Jewish family, was unknown to his generation. Certainly, you could hate your wife, it was expected, but you didn't call a lawyer and let all the relatives find out. If you divorced, what was the advantage? You could only expect to marry another Jewish Princess who would put you through the same hell. The thought that you could marry other than a Jewish Princess never crossed any Jewish husband's mind; the idea that you could find a shiksa to sleep with and not even marry her, that was blasphemy.

Let it be pointed out, however, that the Eleventh Commandment at that time was only hearsay. It was vaguely thought to exist, more by common agreement than any certain knowledge. It appeared nowhere in the Torah, the sacred scrolls in the Ark of every temple, brought forth and chanted on the High Holidays. None of the ancient books spelled it out; if it had been carved into the back side of the Holy Tablets, as had been rumored, the ancient prophets had failed to record it, through either ignorance or design.

Through the ages the Old Testament in the original Aramaic and Hebrew had passed into Greek, and then into Latin, and eventually into English and a hundred other tongues, without any written mention of the most important admonition of all. In the scrolls found in the caves of Qumran, written two thousand years ago, there was no mention of the existence of a hidden commandment other than a cryptic phrase here and there—"cleave to thine wife despite headaches" appeared in one fragment, but the rest of the sentence had turned to dust.

So if it was anything, it was only common law, and certainly not binding on a sovereign government or its citizens.

This was the state of things on the historic night Jacob Schoenbaum decided to drink the Waldorf-Astoria bar dry. He started on the slivovitz, as earlier recorded, and naturally got no further. He poured out his heart to the bartender, who poured out a bottle for Schoenbaum, and by that time they were both half gone. Schoenbaum slid off the barstool and was lying on the floor. This was no condition for a distinguished member of the Cabinet; the bartender called a taxi, and the minister of consumer affairs was taken to his home in Savyon, suffering from too much consumerism.

He was lying on his face on his bed, not having bothered to remove his clothes, when he was nudged into wakefulness by the Voice.

"Schoenbaum!" thundered the Voice. "Awakest thou!"

Schoenbaum rolled over, drunkenly, the room reeling about him. Through the window, in the direction of Bethlehem, he saw three bright stars. Or maybe it was two. Or four. Possibly one. Those who are familiar with slivovitz will understand.

"So who's hollering on Schoenbaum?" he inquired.

"The Lord of Abraham and Isaac and Joseph," said the Voice. "Also Moses and Job and Noah and Ezekiel and—"

"I asked a simple question; don't make from it a federal case," said Schoenbaum, who had developed a headache of his own by now.

"Pay attention, Schoenbaum," thundered the Voice. "Or I'll give you already a bigger headache. Your zayde Yussel told me, from a baby, you were always a nudnik."

Oy, thought Schoenbaum, who could know I have a headache I didn't mention? Who could know my zayde's name was Yussel? Could it be Him? It must be. Who else? He sat up slowly, clutching his forehead.

"Something's wrong?" he inquired. "The reason I didn't go to temple on Yom Kippur, the stomach was upset from fasting; You wouldn't want I got out of a sick bed?"

"So how come thou played pinochle that day?"

Oy, thought Schoenbaum again, it *is* Him.

"That's why I lost?"

"What else?" said the Voice. "Thou shalt not take the name of the Lord thy God in vain, even with four queens and the jack."

"Listen," said Schoenbaum, "stop hollering on me already, and tell me: Am I dead?"

"You got a headache?"

"Yes."

"So don't be a shlimazl, how could you be dead?"

"If I'm not dead, why are You wasting Your time?"

"Sophie sent Me."

It all became clear to Schoenbaum now. Of course. Sophie could tell the Lord what to do in such a nice way, He wouldn't realize she was leading Him by the nose. She must have heard, all the way in heaven. This kind of news travels fast.

"Tell Sophie I tried my best," he said, hunting around for a Manuelo y Vega. "I got Sonya married, a Nice Jewish Boy, a doctor." He didn't mention Chaim was only a Doctor of Oil; maybe the Lord didn't know or at least wouldn't tell Sophie. "What can I do, he's a momzer? Runs three times a week to Gomorrah, an Arab shiksa ought to be ashamed of herself; by the time Chaim gets back home he's as much good to Sonya as a wet latke. You understand?"

"Understand? Who wrote the Song of Solomon? Sammy Cahn? And put out that farshtinkener cigar. It smells to high heaven."

Reluctantly, Schoenbaum put the Manuelo y Vega out in an ashtray; while he never hesitated to fight City Hall, fighting the Celestial Kingdom was something else.

"So now," he said, "Sonya threw him out from the Lincoln bedroom; they're going to be separated a little while."

"Separated?" thundered the Lord. "I heard divorce!"

"If You heard, it's probably true," said Schoenbaum, trapped. He hadn't wanted Sophie to know. A disgrace. Never before, in the whole family.

"Schoenbaum!" thundered Jehovah. "You're not telling everything!"

"Why bother? I thought You knew without telling."

"Of course, but Sophie doesn't believe Me. She wants to hear it from you."

Schoenbaum could understand the problem. He knew Sophie.

"All right," he admitted finally. "Sonya is pregnant by Chaim; she doesn't want to tell him."

"There's more," insisted the Lord.

"I know, but this I can't tell Sophie, it could kill her."

"Tell!" thundered the Lord.

"Such a headache I got," Schoenbaum protested, "would You mind whispering?"

"Schoenbaum," roared the Lord, "tell Sophie what is by Sonya in her mind, or I'll give thou such a headache thou wilt wish thou were by Me downstairs!"

Clouds were obscuring the Bethlehem stars in the night sky, all four or one of them. There was a clap of thunder. Don't tummel with God, Schoenbaum remembered. With Him, every hand is gin.

"Sonya I'm sure doesn't mean it," he insisted, "but what she said is, she would like she shouldn't have the baby, maybe a hot bath, jumping up and down, who knows how girls do it today? All right, I'll say the word: Sonya wants an abortion."

"Oy!" thundered the Lord, although he must have known it all the time.

"You're telling me," said Schoenbaum sadly. "Turn off the lightning already; with this headache a person could go blind."

"Sorry, I couldn't help. Listen, Schoenbaum, this I couldn't tell Sophie."

"So don't."

"But she'll ask, what should I say?"

"So lie a little, what could it hurt?"

"*Me*, lie?"

"I forgot, You got a problem."

Nobody wanted to hurt Sophie. She was that sort of person. And this would hurt her so terribly. A grandchild. It was her dream. Now how could anyone tell her it was being thrown away?

The thunder and lightning had stopped. The Manuelo y Vega had gone out. The room remained in silence. Schoenbaum got to his feet and crossed slowly to the window.

"Listen," he said, "what happened? You still there?"

"I'm thinking," said the Lord. "I don't have a right I should think?"

"Take your time," Schoenbaum answered, hunting for a match. "You mind if I smoke?"

A bolt of lightning hit right near the White House rose garden, followed by a clap of thunder that rattled the windows.

"I was only asking," said Schoenbaum sadly.

"Schoenbaum!" thundered Jehovah. "I don't like this whole thing that's happening in Israel. I could start maybe another flood, a few plagues, but it's bad for My image. Also, could be it's My fault, I didn't explain right to Moses."

"It takes a big person to admit He's wrong," said Schoenbaum.

"Not wrong, but how did I know Moses was such a shlemiel he was too ashamed to tell the Prophets, look at the back side? On the front I should have written it."

"Written what?"

"Never mind. Go by this momzer, Chaim Bernstein, tell him he should drive over to Qumran. On the left he'll find four caves in a cliff; the littlest one, number three, he should take his rock hammer and a shovel. A rock hammer he's got?"

"He'll borrow from Haimowitz," Schoenbaum informed Him.

"Good. He'll crawl into the cave; in the back on the left side he'll find a piece, granite. He knows from granite?"

"From Texas Tech he's got a diploma."

"Oy," said God, "I was hoping maybe MIT."

"He'll find, he'll find," Schoenbaum assured him. "Rocks he understands, women no."

"So he'll find the piece granite; he'll hit with the hammer; it'll break open; in the back he'll find a hole. Dig with the shovel; up will come looks like a piece cement. Pay no attention. Knock with the hammer; the cement will chip off, inside a pot from clay, in the old days they used to make cholent, twenty-four hours it cooked."

"Sophie says twenty-six."

"All right, I'm an expert on cholent? Twenty-six, if Sophie says. Chaim should take the cholent pot to Hebrew University, Jerusalem, give it to Haimowitz. He'll know what to do."

"Haimowitz? The nebbish?"

"When the uniform is off, Haimowitz is A number one. Remember Who said it."

"I wouldn't forget," Schoenbaum assured him. "This is all?"

"Positively."

"Everything will be all right?"

"You want it in black and white, on a piece paper?" thundered Jehovah, incensed.

"In your case I'll make an exception," Schoenbaum assured him, "gladly."

"That's all!"

"Wait!" Schoenbaum was sober now, or at least relatively so. And he knew now how to handle his latest adversary.

"For Sophie's sake, not mine," he said, "what's going to be with Sonya, she's pregnant?"

The Voice of the Lord was softer now.

"Believe Me," He said, "there'll be a grandchild born. For Sophie's sake," He added.

"Boy or girl?" Schoenbaum inquired.

"How should I know?" thundered Jehovah. "Who am I, Walter Cronkite?"

12 Thou Shalt Find the Cholent Pot

IT WAS MORE difficult than Schoenbaum thought it would be. The next morning he drove to the Pinsker Street oilfield, where the guard immediately opened the gate and waved him through. On Pinsker Street, Schoenbaum was king. He noted the gushers were gushing more forcefully than ever; a hundred wells were producing at a tempo never before seen, the tremendous pressure in the underground Schoenbaum continuing to mount. Oil still covered the pavement, overflowing from the wellheads. The feverish activity of the workers, the trucks, the trains, made it all seem like an undercranked old-time silent movie, except for the noise, the roar of the gushers, the clanking of the pumps, the throbbing of the engines, the shouts of the workers. He remembered the night Uncle Zvi had assured him he was making a mistake, buying that forsaken shack. For the first time Schoenbaum thought Zvi might have been right.

In the Pinsker Street Oil Conglomerate headquarters building Schoenbaum was ushered into Chaim's plush, air-conditioned offices by Rivka. Her relationship with her boss had steadily deteriorated. Zivka and Mivka were somewhat concealed beneath a high-necked blouse, although the disguise could never be perfect. The knowledge of their presence still caused faint stirrings in Chaim's memory, despite the path he had worn to Gomorrah, and he secretly hoped one day Rivka would turn herself on. But so far no luck. She resented his excursions into pan-Arabism almost as much as Sonya, who at least had had the advantage of a ceremony.

Rivka stepped out of the office and closed the door, and Schoenbaum immediately got down to business. He was here, he told his son-in-law, not to holler, not to plead for Sonya, but to speak for Israel. As Moses had been summoned to the Mount, so Chaim was being summoned to the cave.

"What are you talking about?" Chaim wanted to know. He glanced at his watch. He was due to hit the road for Gomorrah in fifteen minutes; he had a reservation, but Salome wouldn't keep his place in line forever.

"What I'm talking about," Schoenbaum told him, "is that last night something happened you wouldn't believe. I had a little too much slivovitz, lay down on my bed, right away came lightning, thunder."

"Naturally," Chaim said impatiently. "Slivovitz is at least three hundred proof. And that's the regular, not the high test."

"Wait," said Schoenbaum. "On top of the lightning, the thunder, came a Voice. 'Schoenbaum,' It said, 'go to Chaim Barak, in the caves in Qumran he will find a cholent pot; this he must take to Haimowitz!' "

"Listen, Pop," Chaim said, because he liked the old man, "I know you're upset about Sonya; it can't be helped. I love her, I want her back, but on my terms, not hers. If she can't understand, it's not the end of the world. But I'm not going to give in. I can be a Schoenbaum, too. So calm down."

"Listen, sonny boy," Schoenbaum shouted, "I wouldn't

even talk to a momzer like you, only how could I say no to the Voice? By Bethlehem came stars! In the sky It wrote with lightning! From Western Union you don't get this kind service.''

"Sonya sent you," Chaim decided, "to pretend you're going out of your mind, so I'll feel sorry and go back to her. You can tell her it won't work." He looked at his watch again. "Excuse me," he said, "I have a meeting."

He started to get to his feet.

"Sit down!" ordered his father-in-law. "From this type meeting a fellow can go blind; you don't think I know what's going on?"

"Tell Sonya it won't do any good to threaten me." Chaim was already slipping into his leather jacket.

"Threaten you? Sonya? Never! My daughter doesn't beg! No matter what you did to her, she still wouldn't tell you she's pregnant!''

Chaim-Harold Barak froze, and it wasn't the air conditioning. Schoenbaum, in consternation, realized he had revealed too much.

"Pregnant?" Chaim refused to believe it. "It can't be! I was always careful!''

"You told me where to dig for water, up came oil. By you that's careful?''

Chaim's world was turning upside down. The feeling he had for Sonya was something Salome and her kind could never approach. He had been trying to arouse his wife's jealousy; the fact that he found the way pleasurable was only incidental, in addition to being fatiguing. He knew Salome's passion for him was in direct proportion to her fees. Sonya could never be placed on his American Express card; Sonya was reality, and reality is never easy or simple, like the girls at the Pillar of Salt Playboy Club. Although he pretended otherwise to Schoenbaum, Chaim had often been on the point of throwing in the towel and going back to his wife on her own terms. He had only been trying to teach Sonya a lesson: Stop being a Jewish Princess and match the competition.

Now she had not only matched but surpassed it, in a way the entire staff of the seraglio in Gomorrah could not equal. Not that they could not become pregnant; only a constant state of careful kept them unpregnant, considering the opportunities. No, it wasn't that.

What Chaim-Harold had never admitted to himself was that someday he wanted to have a son. And no son of his could be half Arab. That was unthinkable.

In a land as old as any on this globe, one race, one tribe, had endured. Enslaved by the Romans, dispersed over the face of the earth during the Diaspora, decimated by the Inquisition, murdered by the Nazis, attacked by the Arabs with the tacit approval of the British, betrayed by the French, alternately aided and hindered by the Americans, one race had continued to survive in the homeland of its fathers. One reason had been that its fathers and its mothers had been of the same scorned people, at least often enough to prolong the characteristics that set them apart from the rest of humanity. They suffered for being different, and this same differentness was their hope and their salvation and their unifying force.

Chaim-Harold had come to Israel because he was Jewish. To have a child who was not would be to deny two thousand years of tragic and triumphant history.

His son would have to go through all the pain and tsuris of growing up Jewish that his father had endured, from the bris to the bar mitzvah that set him apart from the other boys in Dallas, Texas, so that father and son could understand each other. How else was understanding possible? Jewish guilt was something precious, the feeling that when you are God's chosen, you will arouse His wrath more often than others; otherwise, why should His people have to suffer every time they enjoyed life too much? It was a bond no outsider could appreciate.

It was this guilt, this understanding of being special, that had made the tiny, vulnerable nation of Israel possible. Chaim could never take the one certain way of destroying it. No; Chaim-Harold Barak-Bernstein, Junior, could not be half an Arab.

Harold did not realize that by admitting this openly to himself, he was helping defeat Plan C, which was then proceeding exactly as the PLO and the Arab League had hoped, although no one in Israel had heard of it yet. It would be some time before Shemuhl Kishner would report his secret intelligence to the Prime Minister and the Cabinet.

"My God," said Chaim, sitting down again at his desk. "When is she going to have my son?"

"Maybe never," Schoenbaum informed him. "Sonya is talking already hot baths, with Epsom salts."

"I'll kill her!" Chaim had leaped to his feet. "It's half mine; she has no right! At least she should ask me first!"

"Every time before you run to Gomorrah you ask perhaps her permission?"

"It's not the same!"

"So what's different for a man, except the Arab shiksa doesn't get a headache?"

Chaim considered that. It had the ring of truth.

"How can we stop Sonya?" he asked finally.

Schoenbaum crossed to him and pointed a finger. When Schoenbaum pointed a finger, the world listened.

"I made a deal, you give to Haimowitz the cholent pot from Qumran, Sonya will go ahead, have the baby."

"Sonya promised?"

"Not Sonya, the Voice."

"Oh, Christ," said Chaim.

"Please," Schoenbaum requested. "You couldn't say instead 'Holy Moses'?"

Chaim-Harold got to his feet and crossed to the window, hands shoved into his pockets. "Schoenbaum, you're an old man, you've gone senile."

"Bite your tongue!" said Schoenbaum. But it hit home. Seventy-five years old. He had wondered many times if perhaps he could no longer cope, especially after Sophie left. He had fought old age as long as he could. He was tired of fighting. Maybe last night his tummeling mind had finally given up. In the light of day it seemed possible. Nay, probable. He turned away, already growing older.

Chaim noticed his hesitation.

"See?" he said. "I'm right! Voices! Lightning! Stars by Bethlehem! Schoenbaum, you're a fool! You've become an alter kocker!"

Unnoticed, the east had been clouding over. There was a distant rumbling, then a flash of lightning and a deafening clap of thunder that almost shattered the window in Chaim's face.

"Schmuck!" the lightning blazoned across the skies from horizon to horizon. "GO ALREADY!"

13 A Majority of One

SOMETIME EARLY in 1947 a group of Bedouin nomads was engaged in smuggling goats and other contraband out of what was then Transjordan into Palestine. They had moved far south of the Allenby Bridge and were preparing to float their goods across the river, safe from the eyes and the guns of the British guards. They paused in the desert near the Dead Sea to fill their water bags at the spring of En Feshka, when a young Bedouin boy, who was herding the goats nearby, noticed that one of them had wandered off, as goats and Chaim Baraks are wont to do. The young shepherd was called Muhammad the Wolf, and he was not about to be outsmarted by a mere nameless goat. He chased after it and made an accidental discovery that not even the greatest archaeologists had been able to achieve on purpose.

The goat, led by some nameless impulse, had climbed up a cliff just below the opening to a cave Muhammad the Wolf had never before noticed. Muhammad threw a rock at the goat and missed; if he had had the accuracy of a Don Sutton or even Mark Fidrych, he would have hit the goat and eliminated his place in history. Instead, he threw the rock high and outside, and it went through the opening of the cave; but instead of rolling to some invisible backstop, it apparently smashed something fragile within, and the sound of the crash wafted to Muhammad's ears. Like all small boys who have ever hurled a ball through a neighbor's window, Muhammad ran. He ran doubly fast because he knew there couldn't be any neighbor in that cave. No one had lived there for thousands of years. If he had hit anything, it had to be the property of an evil spirit, who would not be satisfied to call a cop or Muhammad's father; the spirit was quite capable of destroying Muhammad's soul and his body before Muhammad could explain he hadn't been warmed up and his fastball had gotten away from him.

Muhammad scrambled and rolled to the bottom of the cliff and then, to his surprise, discovered he was still alive. If he was alive, there wasn't an evil spirit in the cave. Like all small boys, his next reaction was one of curiosity. What had he broken? Muhammad whistled up a neighboring shepherd, another small boy whose name is not recorded, which shows how unimportant it is to be merely an accomplice to a historical event, and together they climbed back to the cave and started to find out what Muhammad had shattered.

It turned out to be an old clay jar, among a lot of other old clay jars and fragments of pottery. There were lids on the jars, and when they took them off, whatever was inside smelled very bad, which, to small boys, made them very interesting. What smelled, it turned out, were oblong lumps wrapped up in lengths of old linen, covered with a coating of something black. From the smell, they were not edible. Muhammad and his friend took them outside, where the fresh air was a welcome change, and started to investigate the mystery. They were so disappointed when they unwrapped the lengths of linen and found out they held neither gold nor rubies nor diamonds, and rubbing the jars produced no magic genie, that they almost threw the contents away. If you couldn't find the *Arabian Nights* in Arabia, where could you find them? All that was inside the linen was some old rolls of writing they couldn't read, written in parallel columns on thin sheets of some kind of leather that had been sewn together and was crumbling to bits in their fingers.

The others in the party had finished filling the water bags and called to the boys to come down from the cliff; Muhammad and his friend knew they would have to explain why they had deserted their goats, so they brought some of the smelly old parchments down with them. Their elders couldn't read them either, but it was decided to take them along to Bethlehem, where perhaps they could pass them off on some antique dealer who could then pass them off on some tourist. For centuries the Bedouin had been selling pieces of the true cross in this way, for a very good price. Indeed, when business became good, they had set up a true cross factory that produced not only wholesale fragments of the original crucifix but also the nails, the crown of thorns, and even a few faded old photographs of the actual event, which didn't sell too well.

In Bethlehem nobody could read the writing on the parchment, and besides, the tourists were becoming a little more wary since several pairs of the authentic sandals worn by Jesus were discovered to contain the legend "Made in Czechoslovakia."

The Bedouin shlepped the scrolls all the way to Jerusalem, where the Metropolitan of Jerusalem—an archbishop, not a museum—expressed an interest, because he knew that no one who could write had lived anywhere near En Feshkha since the first Christian centuries, when the En Feshkha real estate bubble had collapsed. The Metropolitan also knew there was only one man who might decipher the strange writing: Professor Sukenik of the Hebrew University. But there was a problem; war was about to break out, the war which was to become known as the War of Liberation but should really have been called the First War of Liberation, and no one could expect Professor Sukenik to cross into enemy territory to read an old, smelly piece of parchment. At this time, the British army, which ruled Palestine, was preventing Jewish refugees from landing, and the Jewish underground army was retaliating. There had been killings and bombings and a spectacular rescue of Jewish prisoners from jail; the Jewish sections of Jerusalem were under martial law. Soon the British were to pull out and full-scale war between Arab and Jew was to begin.

So, naturally, Professor Sukenik, being Professor Sukenik, risked his life three times a week to make his way through enemy lines and into Bethlehem and the forbidden sections of Jerusalem, just to examine the crumbling leather scrolls Muhammad the Wolf had found in the cave of Qumran. In the midst of the battle for Jerusalem, with shells falling all about, he held a press conference for foreign correspondents to announce, with tears in his eyes, the discovery of the oldest Hebrew manuscripts known to humanity, dating to the first or second century before Christ and containing strange sections that do not appear in any of the Bibles handed down through the ages. The parchments had been written by the Essenes, an ancient tribe of priests who practiced continence, did not allow women to join the order, and maintained a successful, carefree male society that had no births and no children. So many men on the outside were anxious to flee their families and join the happy priesthood that their numbers kept increasing steadily over the years. Supposedly, the Essenes were destroyed in their caves by the Roman legions who conquered all ancient Palestine, but there have been rumors that the women of Palestine supplied the Romans with maps and encouragement and even pointed out the way.

It was to En Feshkha that Chaim Barak drove his Mercedes. The area of the Dead Sea caves is now in the territory of Israel, not Jordan, and it has been opened to the public as a historical monument. Supposedly, all its treasures have long since been carted off and deposited in the museums of the world; all its secrets have been photographed and translated; all its scrolls have been studied and evaluated. Chaim-Harold knew all this. He also knew it was quite possible the lightning flash that had commanded him to come here had been a mere figment of his fevered imagination. But he was in no mood to gamble.

Chaim was not religious; he did not believe in God, but he did believe in hedging his bets. If there were an Almighty, it might be a good idea to give Him the benefit of the doubt. And if this were a wild-goose chase, all Chaim would lose was an afternoon, not his eternal soul. The odds were favorable. Jimmy the Greek would have approved.

From the car Chaim took out a knapsack containing his prospecting tools and slung it on his back. He was wearing his army fatigues and almost blended into the sand. He started hiking up the path built for the tourists and saw above him the row of ancient caves, shimmering in the desert heat. Four caves, with the smallest the third from the left. The path ended far below the cave, and Chaim had to clamber up the almost sheer side of the cliff where Muhammad the Wolf had thrown his fastball, in order to haul himself through the opening. He took out his flashlight and surveyed the interior of the cave, a mass of rocks and sand turned over several times by the archaeologists who had preceded him. There were a few shards of pottery visible, but that was all. Foolish, Chaim thought, a hundred diggers have gone through this a dozen times, it's hot, why waste time in here breaking rocks? I'll tell Schoenbaum I looked, found nothing. He turned back for the entrance.

"Chaim Barak!" boomed the Voice. *"Come back!"*

Chaim turned, startled. A trick, he thought. Someone's wired the cave for sound, to give me a good scare. But who? Or Who? Why take a chance? He flashed his light about the gloomy interior. Over in one corner, where the top of the cave slanted down, he saw an outcropping of rock. He got down on his knees and crawled to it, then pulled his rock hammer out of his pack. He took out a chisel and started to chip away at the base expertly. In a few minutes Chaim had worked the rock loose and managed to roll it to one side. Behind it, more rock.

"Shmuck!" boomed the Voice again. "This is by you granite? Go back to class!"

Chaim turned the flashlight on the rock again. "Oops, sorry," he said, "it's feldspar. I guess I made a mistake."

"Texas Tech," moaned the Voice. "Why should I have all the lousy luck?"

"Wait!" said Chaim. "I see it! I see it!"

The flashlight had picked up a section of the rock wall of the cave that seemed to be inlaid; an irregular piece of granite had been set into the contrasting stone.

"Congratulations," the Voice boomed. "Don't hit the thumb."

Chaim nodded and went to work. Carefully, he made a notch in the hard granite at the point where it joined the rest of the wall face. Inserting another chisel, he levered against it, until finally the granite was worked loose to the point where he could grab it with his hands. He forced it out of the wall, sideways like the door of a wall safe, and carefully set it down. Taking the flashlight, he turned it on the opening. The beam of light revealed a tiny cavern; within it, a large piece of pottery, covered with what had once been mortar to protect it from the ravages of time. It was black with age.

Chaim set the flashlight down inside to illuminate the little cave. No human being had looked within for two millennia.

"*Baruch atah adonoy,*" he mumbled. It was all he remembered, so it had to serve the occasion. "*Elohanu melech hoalim,*" he concluded.

"Shlimazl!" boomed the Voice again. "That's the prayer for wine."

"It's the only prayer I know," Chaim admitted; "otherwise, I would have prayed for scotch. I could use some."

The Voice merely groaned.

With trembling hands, Chaim reached into the cavern and

picked up the mortar-encrusted cholent pot. Reverently, he shook the sand off it and got to his feet. His head hit the top of the cave, and he dropped the pot on the rock floor.

"Oy!" boomed the Voice, more in sorrow than anger.

"Sorry," Chaim said again, picking the pot up to see if it had been damaged. Fortunately, it was intact. He crawled to the opening in the cave and started to lower himself outside.

"Chaim!" The Voice sounded pained. "The flashlight! Thou wants to ruin maybe the batteries?"

Chaim would have cursed softly under his breath, but he was afraid that somehow the Voice was tuned in to his thoughts. He crawled back to the hole in the cave wall and retrieved the lighted flashlight. Returning to the entrance to the cave, he once more started to lower himself outside.

"Don't forget," the Voice commanded, "take it to Haimowitz right away, don't stop by Gomorrah, or there'll be *two* pillars from salt!"

Chaim nodded sadly. Big Daddy was watching him.

It was a small but select group that gathered in the geology laboratory of the Hebrew University in Jerusalem to watch Professor Haimowitz, in complete command of the situation now that he was in civilian clothes, carefully chip the mortar away and delicately lift off the top of the cholent pot to reveal the ancient linen-wrapped object within. Chaim, Schoenbaum, and the chief rabbi of Jerusalem watched as Haimowitz and two of his students carefully unwrapped the find, the crumbling parchment roll that lay within the linen and wax covering, as it had since before the birth of Jesus Christ. The odor that assailed their nostrils was the same that had turned the stomachs of Muhammad the Wolf and his little friend, but to the group in the laboratory it was holy, the smell of time itself, not just a putrefying goatskin parchment.

Gently, carefully, the scroll, which seemed to be in excellent condition, was unrolled with the aid of special tongs under the lights that had been set up to photograph it. An assistant was clicking a camera. Reverently, they all regarded the blackened object that was being stretched out on the laboratory table. It was unlike any of the scrolls seen before. Instead of the parallel rows of ancient writing stretching from top to bottom, there were a series of lines, some vertical, some horizontal. At the top of the parchment, two of the lines came to a point. There was a moment of puzzlement. Finally, Haimowitz spoke in a voice choked with emotion.

"Gentlemen," he said, "we are looking at a drawing of the Holy Tablets, possibly made from life."

The others gasped. Now that Haimowitz had given the clue they could all see it. The straight lines were the sides of the tablets. The lines coming to a point were their peaked tops. The ancient lettering in the middle was, to them, indecipherable; but to Haimowitz, it was *McGuffey's Reader*.

"It is in the language of the Essene," he said, "and the writing here at the top is simple. What it says is: 'Thou shalt have no other God before me.' And here, extending from the top to the bottom, are all the rest, ending with the tenth, 'Thou shalt not covet thy neighbor's wife,' which is underlined twice. There is no question that the parchment is priceless. It must go immediately to the Hebrew Museum."

There was hushed approval. Carefully, gently, Haimowitz started to roll the parchment back once more to its original form.

"SHMUCK!" thundered a Voice. "TURN IT OVER!"

Startled, the professor almost dropped the precious relic off the table; only his assistants managed to save it at the last moment. There was absolute quiet now, for the atmosphere had become one close to terror. The Voice had been heard by all. There was no longer any question of its being an illusion.

With trembling hands, Haimowitz unrolled the blackened document once more and, with the aid of his assistants, carefully turned it over. There, on the back side, now that they knew what they were looking for, the drawing was plainly visible: the faint lines indicating the rear of a tablet and, in huge lettering covering the entire surface, as if Whoever had written it were consumed with anger, the words in ancient Aramaic which Haimowitz stammeringly translated for his frightened audience: "Eleven. THOU SHALT NOT SHTUP A SHIKSA!"

Frightened silence, as the import of the moment sank in.

"Is there a telephone here?" Chaim Barak inquired, his voice cracking like an adolescent's. "I have to cancel an appointment."

Prime Minister Meir received a visitor that afternoon in the Jerusalem offices of the Israeli government, a visitor she had not expected. It was Israel's former Chief of State, looking trim and rested after his long vacation in the mountains. He was accompanied by Aluf Shimon Gan, chief of intelligence. Golda, startled, got up, forgetting that she had removed her Ferragamo shoes under the desk, and started forward to greet her predecessor in her stockinged feet before she realized her error.

"Excuse me," she said, "I forgot, the new shoes are a little tight, I was letting the feet breathe." She blew a wisp of her blond hair out of her eyes and extended her hand to the former Prime Minister in greeting.

"You're looking good," she said. "I'm so happy."

"Golda," he told her, "I wouldn't have recognized you. In that tight pants suit you look like an old Dizengoff Street nafka."

"It's the latest. You don't want the Prime Minister to be up to date? I'm setting an example."

"I've seen enough of the example. The whole country has gone crazy. I came back from Mount Hermon to see if all the stories were true. I couldn't believe what I was hearing on my radio and seeing on the television from Kol Israel." He started to pace, a bad sign, Golda knew.

"Nobody's paying taxes; everybody's running around. Playboy Clubs, Maxims, in the back room Temple Beth Hillel just opened a massage parlor. When I talk to my friends, they say, 'What do you expect? Goldie Myerson drives in a Rolls-Royce.'"

"It really comes out cheaper," Golda insisted. "In two years the government can sell it used for more than it cost new, you'll see."

"You'll sell it *tomorrow*. The government of Israel is not in the used car business."

Golda's chin set in a firm line.

"Never tummel with a tummler," she said. "You left; you couldn't handle Schoenbaum; I managed the whole thing. I am still the Prime Minister."

"Not for long," he told her, "when I give the Cabinet the information Shimon brought me."

Golda whirled on her intelligence chief. "Shimon! You have secret intelligence, so you should bring it to the Prime Minister, not somebody who's not in the government anymore!"

Shimon was not a man to be intimidated, even by so formidable a tummler as Mrs. Meir.

"I tried to," he said, "but you were at the beauty parlor, under the dryer. I waited two hours. Your secretary told me the toenails were being painted."

Golda tried to brazen it out. "You want a Prime Minister should walk around with naked toenails?" she demanded.

Her predecessor crossed and took her by the shoulders, not unkindly. "Golda," he said, "remember me? I'm your friend. We've gone through too much together. Can't you understand what being Prime Minister of a country like Israel does to you? I'm a tough old soldier, but twice, I've almost had a breakdown. You're a woman, a strong woman, but a woman; don't you realize what has been happening to you?"

He turned her so she could see her image in a mirror on the wall. The Cardin blouse. The St. Laurent pants. The blond hair. The silicone.

"My God," said Golda, as it hit her at last, "I look *goyish!*"

He nodded.

"You see?" he said. "They did to you what they're trying to do to the rest of the country."

"If they could make *me* look goyish," said Golda, "the rest of the country is easy."

"Of course. They couldn't beat us on the battlefield, so they're doing it in the beauty parlor and the bedroom."

"The bedroom? How the bedroom?" Golda was puzzled.

Her predecessor turned to his chief of intelligence. "Tell her, Shimon," he ordered.

"Plan C," Shimon Gan told Golda, "was decided upon as soon as news of the Pinsker Street Gusher was confirmed in Damascus. Shemuhl Kishner sent Nadya Haffaz to Cairo to get further information. She wormed her way into the bedroom of Anwar el-Sadat himself."

Golda was trying to visualize Nadya worming her way into anything smaller than a boxcar when Shimon enlightened her.

"She wormed her way in by breaking down the door," he explained. "Sadat was asleep, and when Nadya, who is not very subtle, tried to climb into bed with him, he jumped out the window. It seems he had just attended the Egyptian premiere of *King Kong* and wasn't taking any chances. Nadya had a bugging device concealed on her person, I would be embarrassed to tell you where, but since it was Nadya's person, it was possible to hide a radio transmitter. This she placed in the chandelier, she got the idea from an old Ray Milland movie she saw on television, and then she escaped."

"Wait," said Golda, who had gone along with the whole story up to this point. "How could Nadya escape?"

"It's not exactly clear, but in her debriefing she said something about the soldiers who arrested her being little more than boys, there were only five of them, they were very curious, and she was able to bribe them.''

''With what?''

''Please,'' said Shimon, ''I never ask Nadya that, I have a weak stomach.''

''From the hidden transmitter,'' the former leader continued the story while Shimon Gan attempted to control his queasiness, ''we learned that Plan C was a concerted effort to undermine Israel. First, by withdrawing the tanks of Plan B. Without an enemy, without somebody shooting at them, our people feel uncomfortable. Then they start to relax. For our people, relaxing is not normal. They become soft, gentle, sometimes almost lovable.''

''Oy,'' said the Prime Minister, realizing the extent of the damage for the first time.

''Then,'' her informant continued, ''without taxes, with money all over, with time on their hands, they started to think about women. Our girls have been able to get away with being Jewish Princesses for so long because nobody had time to think about it. Every man was always busy, had to get back to the store or to the office or to the army; if it's a girl, grab, if you have to marry, marry. If you wasted time thinking is she pretty, do I want to live with her the rest of my life, how will she be in bed, the Arabs would start shooting, it could be too late. Plan C was to give our men time to think, and while they were thinking, send in Arab girls so they could stop thinking and start doing.''

''That's the whole reasoning behind the harems?''

''Oh, no.'' By this time Shimon felt better and was able to resume presenting his information. ''The harems were part only of a larger plan. Once our men got used to the idea—girls you didn't have to marry even, taking orders they enjoyed, actually—the second phase was to begin. Headaches the Arab girls would start to get.''

''They were operating as secret agents?'' Golda wanted to know.

Shimon nodded. "For the PLO. First, headaches; next, nagging would start. 'What's the matter, an Arab girl isn't good enough to marry?' 'You want me to keep doing this for you, just for your pleasure? What about mine?' 'Listen, I'm a nice girl; first, the ring.' "

"They might as well be Jewish," Golda reasoned.

"Exactly. But also they were better looking, better trained, and would do things like no Nice Jewish Girl would allow."

"You might say it was an attack from the rear," added his companion. "It was hoped our men would marry these Arab girls under stress and, in the natural course of things, have half-Arab children. So the Palestinians would be returning to Israel, I almost said through the back door."

"I'm glad you didn't," Golda told him. She had been such a fool, not to recognize the purpose, the danger, the enemy. It was the dilution of the race, the race that had endured so long because of its differentness; to destroy the one glue that held the nation together. In the Hebrew religion, Jewishness is passed down traditionally only from the mother, the patriarchs in their wisdom subscribing to the doctrine that it is a wise child who knows his own father, and a wiser mother who doesn't tell him. Thus, all the half-Jewish children born to the Arab girls would, by Jewish law, be legally considered Arab. In a generation or two the invasion of the bedroom would succeed in surrendering Israel without a fight, except for the occasional disagreement over who was to lie on top.

Plan C was fiendishly clever; it was the kind of defeat a whole army could relax and enjoy.

Something had to be done immediately. But what?

It was at that moment the telephone rang. It was Schoenbaum.

"Golda!" he hollered. "Call a meeting already from the Cabinet, mine son the doctor has just discovered—" He stopped. The Prime Minister could hear a whispered conversation at the other end of the line. "Mine son the doctor and his friend the nebbish have made a discovery!"

The Golda Meir who made the opening announcement at the Cabinet meeting that night was a different woman. The change in her appearance was as dramatic as her announcement itself. She had exchanged her Cardin pants suit for an old shmatta of a dress, the tight shoes for comfortable herring boxes, and while it would take her hair a while to grow in gray, Golda was starting to look again like the wise old bubba who had brought her nation through crisis after crisis.

But this one was too much for her.

"I have been very foolish," she told her old friends. "I fell into a trap carefully planned by the enemy. For us, there can be no easy road to peace and prosperity. We were conceived in pain and created in sorrow, and it is only through adversity that we can continue to exist. In the few years it will take for the Pinsker Street Gusher to become a trickle, the fabric of our ancient race could be completely destroyed. We must call a halt. After enduring so much for so long, after enduring as one people for so long, we cannot, we must not, be seduced by petrodollars and easy tochis into a course that can only end in oblivion. I have taken the first steps. The Rolls-Royce has already been repossessed; the uplift bra, excuse the expression, has been let out; the Lear Jet was only rented anyway. All that is left is for me to turn back the office of Prime Minister in the hope that you will be wise enough to return it to our former leader. We are at war."

There were tears in her eyes, but nothing the members of the Cabinet could say could sway the grand old lady from her course. Besides, the malaise of the country was now felt by all. If it was war, it was the strangest war in their history. The bedroom door had, somehow, to be slammed shut against the seductive enemy. A new leader was needed to accomplish this, and within the hour her predecessor was summoned to regain his post by acclamation, including two shrugs.

"I don't know if I should thank you," he told his Cabinet, "because what we must do will not be easy. If even Golda Meir, in her goodness and her greatness, could not accomplish it, I have doubts of my own ability. Our people have grown used to luxury. It will be difficult for them to accept the stern measures we will be forced to take. However, our task will be eased by the momentous discovery made in the caves above En Feshkha by Schoenbaum's son-in-law, the distinguished manager of the Pinsker Street Oil Conglomerate, what's-his-name.''

He indicated Chaim, who immediately got to his feet and acknowledged the tremendous lack of applause. Chaim had never been very popular since Schoenbaum had forced him into a high-paying job for which every other member of the Cabinet had a son-in-law equally as well qualified for. Nevertheless, this was a moment when they had to acknowledge his achievement, for he had brought large blowups of the photographs of the latest Qumran scroll. He placed them on an easel at the front of the meeting room.

"Gentlemen," he said, "this is a hitherto unknown parchment containing a hitherto unknown portion of the Torah handed to Moses on the Mount, according to legend and the Bible. It indicates that there was a hitherto unknown commandment inscribed on the tablets' rear end.''

"Back side,'' corrected Haimowitz, whose nebbishness was disappearing now that the importance of this discovery was about to receive worldwide acclaim.

"Back side,'' accepted Chaim-Harold, with a condescending nod, "hitherto unknown." He liked that phrase. Most of the acclaim would be his, he knew, since no one but the Lord was aware Chaim had looked under the feldspar first. "It states, in unequivocal terms, 'Eleven. Thou Shalt Not Shtup a Shiksa!' ''

There was a murmur of surprise from the Cabinet; one would almost have said "of guilt,'' but the evidence is still inconclusive, most of it in the files of the American Express Company under the Pillar of Salt Playboy Club account.

"You're sure?'' inquired the minister of the interior, who had a second charge account at the Immaculate Conception

Outcall and was looking for an excuse to stop his check. He was seventy-four years old and felt he should never have agreed to a weekly rate.

"Absolutely!" said Haimowitz, blinking rapidly. He had just arranged for a satellite appearance with Barbara Walters to announce the Qumran discovery and was practicing wearing contact lenses. He got to his feet and crossed to the easel, indicating the writing.

"This is the Aramaic script of the Essene prophets," he explained. "The parchment has been carbon-dated to the first century before Christ. You will note the Aramaic asterisk over here—" He indicated a strange character in the lettering.

"This refers to a notation at the bottom of the scroll." He indicated an ancient scrawl at the bottom of the manuscript, obviously written in some haste. "It reads, 'Top Secret Parchment. Not to be taken from this office.'" He turned back to his listeners. "There is evidence that the chief scribe of the Essene sect, one of their highest priests, whose writing style is evident throughout this entire scroll, had violated his oath of continence with a young and attractive Arab girl who brought the priests water from the spring of En Feshkha. His excuse was that even a prophet can get tired of goats."

He wondered about mentioning this delicate fact on the Barbara Walters program television broadcast; he would probably have to clear it with the ABC network's continuity acceptance. Already Haimowitz was thinking like a star.

"Therefore," he said, "the chief scribe gave orders that this particular commandment was not to be copied further, and it does not appear in any of the biblical texts that were passed down to posterity. While all of us felt such an admonition against indiscriminate shtupping must exist, it never was considered a binding portion of the Mosaic Law, like the one against bacon."

"Furthermore, gentlemen"—Chaim-Harold took over, fearful of Haimowitz's stealing all the thunder—"our Religious Party, through the chief rabbi of Jerusalem, has already accepted this commandment as the authentic word of God and is incorporating it into the scrolls kept in the Holy Ark. They have demanded that it be promulgated by this Cabinet and approved by the Knesset as the law of the land.''

There was a murmur of outrage at this; the Religious Party, whose votes were necessary to keep any Prime Minister in office, was using the leverage of its powerful minority vote to influence national legislation. There was considerable resistance; several ministers intimated the Religious Party had fabricated the parchment to promote its own interests.

"Not so fast!" It was Schoenbaum, on his feet immediately. "Last night came by me a Voice, by Bethlehem came stars, in the sky was writing by lightning! Does this sound like the shlemiels from the Religious Party? Impossible! Maybe with God is only one vote, but by me He's a majority.''

Almost as if in support of his position, the skies to the east had begun to cloud over, and a distant rumble of thunder was heard.

Golda asked for permission to speak unofficially; now that she was no longer Prime Minister, no one could accuse her of having any political motive. All she was concerned with was the good of the people of Israel.

"It should be obvious to all of us by now that the Lord was teaching our people a lesson, as He did at the time of Sodom and Gomorrah, as He did in the time of the Flood. The lesson is to be content to struggle and to suffer, because that is what life is; we are all of us tummlers on the road to eternity, and without tummeling our existence has no meaning. For our people, to endure is what is important, not to drive Rolls-Royces and wear uplift bras, excuse the expression. The fact that we have endured for so long as one race, that is our immortality. The Pinsker Street Gusher and the events that followed have endangered that existence; we have been tempted, and we have been weak. Now we are being commanded to change our ways and preserve our identity. Are we so foolish that we have not learned? The Religious Party is right, maybe for the first time. You must recommend that the law be passed.''

She sat down and exchanged a glance with Schoenbaum. Golda knew what it meant to him; if the law passed, perhaps Harold and Sonya would be reunited. And if they were, perhaps the grandson could be saved. That was all Schoenbaum wanted. It was probably, he thought, what Sonya wanted, despite her anger. Since it was also what Sophie wanted, Schoenbaum was sure she would get Jehovah to go along.

As for Israel, both its men and its women would be brought to their senses. That the Lord had interdicted the Pillar of Salt Playboy Club and the Immaculate Conception Outcall at the moment he had given the tablets to Moses on the Mount spoke well for his foresight as well as his insight. No one could doubt His power. With shiksas forbidden, Jewish men would have to make do with what was at hand at home; the race would be preserved, although some of the fun would have gone out of it. You win a few, you lose a few. The unhappy history of the Jewish people.

By a unanimous vote, without even two shrugs, the Cabinet recommended to the Knesset that the Eleventh Commandment be given the force of law.

Outside the windows the skies cleared. The sun came out. And the voice of the turtle was heard in the land.

Schoenbaum knew he would have a grandson soon. The Lord was putty in Sophie's hands.

14 The Pinsker Street Cover-Up

SONYA   SCHOENBAUM   BARAK-BERN-
STEIN was seated in the Lincoln bathtub reading a book,
hot Epsom salts bubbling in the water that was up to her
middle, when her father suddenly knocked on the door. Startled, she dropped her copy of *The Liberated Woman's Do-It-
Yourself Home Abortion Guide* into the water and had to splash
around frantically to retrieve it, somewhat damp and limp, but
still defiantly legible. This was her fourteenth attempt with hot
Epsom salts; Sonya was still pregnant but pleasantly pink. The
guide appeared to be hastily written. Perhaps Sonya was relieved; she had to go through the motions of owning her own
body, if only to maintain her position with the Sarah Lawrence
Alumnae Association, but she wasn't certain she wanted her
motions to succeed. That was the reason she didn't seek professional medical assistance, readily available in Israel, where
in some areas the doctors outnumber the patients. What Sonya
secretly hoped was that Chaim-Harold would come back to her
to save their child.

"Sonya," Schoenbaum's voice called to her happily, "Chaim-Harold has come back to you to save your child!"

"Tell that momzer to drop dead," she replied immediately, Jewish Princesshood taking precedence over true love for the moment. Secretly, she hoped this response would result in Chaim-Harold's dropping to his knees and pleading for forgiveness through the keyhole.

"Sonya!" It was Chaim's voice, all right, but he still seemed to be standing upright. "You stop the Epsom salts bit and save my son or I'll go to Gomorrah eight times a week, including matinees!"

"Don't threaten me with your heart attack," Sonya replied. "Your eyes were always bigger than your stomach." Although her own heart was aching for him, she could not relinquish her prerogatives. She was the Princess; he was the Frog. The minute he admitted her royal Jewish superiority, achieved by the women of her race by dint of hard work and constant nagging over fifty centuries, she would touch him with her scepter, and he would be her handsome lover once more. All he had to do was pronounce the magic words, "You're Absolutely Right," and keep pronouncing them for the rest of his life.

She listened, hopefully. Nothing. Footsteps. Receding footsteps.

"Chaim!" she called out fearfully, starting to climb out of the tub.

"He's gone," Schoenbaum told her through the door, reproachfully. "Sonya, get out of the tub, stop with the Epsom salts, quick, put on a towel, run after him!"

Sonya stopped short. Her father, too, she remembered, was a man.

"I'd rather die," she said, and slid back into the bubbles, her anger returned. She dried off her *Home Abortion Guide* with the edge of a towel and resumed reading. Maybe, in the next chapter, the author might come up with a gem.

Seething with male wrath, Chaim-Harold drove toward his luxurious offices on Pinsker Street. He had made the gesture, and he had been repulsed. Never would he lower himself to mere Jewish Froghood. In spite of the new law that had just been promulgated, he was thinking seriously of carrying out his threat to return to Gomorrah; it would serve Sonya right. The fears of yesterday had vanished. In the light of his new preeminence because of his discovery in the Qumran caves, Chaim-Harold had dreams of being elevated in the minds of the Israeli public to a position beside Yigael Yadin as one of the nation's great archaeologists. Possibly, in a few years, he might run for Prime Minister. He felt, somehow, that he was now above the law, a mood that seems to flow naturally from even the contemplation of public office these days. He was jolted back to earth when he attempted to drive through the main gate at the Pinsker Street oilfields. He nodded condescendingly to the corporal on guard and waited for the gates to be opened. Nothing. Impatiently, he leaned on the horn of his four-door Mercedes. The corporal brought his rifle to his shoulder and ordered Chaim to get the hell off government property. As Chaim shouted he would report the incident to Schoenbaum, the Cabinet, and the commander in chief of the Israeli Defense Forces, the guard fired a warning shot over the top of the Mercedes, and almost at the same time two of the huge oil derricks visible from the gate were blasted into the air by explosives and fell over on their sides. Then two more. And two more.

Bewildered, Chaim-Harold backed up. The Mercedes was becoming splattered with oil, and Chaim needed a moment to reflect. Should he believe the guard's warning? Should he ignore it and try to get to his office? Should he call for help from his father-in-law? Should he? Shouldn't he? Was this part of a new plan, the Pinsker Street Cover-up? What should he do? Like most men before him in positions of power, in and out of government, Chaim-Harold had one sensible solution when faced with the insoluble: Get laid.

He turned the Mercedes around and headed for the Pillar of Salt Playboy Club, knowing in his heart that it was Sonya's fault.

It was a long drive from Tel Aviv, but visions of Salome in and out of her seven veils—in the interest of historical accuracy, Chaim had bought her a complete set—kept him from being bored. He almost passed Gomorrah without realizing it. As he turned around and headed back toward the Playboy Club, he realized why he had made such an obvious error. In the lot adjoining the Chamber of Commerce, the huge tent had been lowered to the ground. Trucks had been backed up to take the camels and their Bedouin herders back to the desert of the Negev which was their home. The Persian rugs were rolled up, the incense burners turned off, the ceiling mirrors crated, the satin pillows stacked up, and a large packing case full of electric vibrators was on its way to be dumped into the Dead Sea.

Farewell to arms.

Chaim braked the Mercedes to a screeching halt and jumped out. He looked around for Salome and the other Hugging Bunnies but didn't spot them anywhere. Then he noticed, at one side of the field, a dilapidated bus labeled "Kibbutz Kfar Yehuda." A group of girls in ill-fitting shmattas was climbing aboard, carrying cardboard boxes and brown paper bags containing their belongings. In spite of her shabby dress, he recognized Salome instantly from the rear. She was just settling into her seat by an open window when Chaim ran up to the bus, out of breath.

"O moon of my delight," he panted, for this was his customary greeting. It helped both of them get into the mood. "What the hell are you doing in that bus?"

Salome turned her face toward him, and he saw that she was

wearing no makeup. No kohl around her eyes. No ocher accenting the cheeks. Chaim noticed for the first time that she had pimples. On her face. They certainly weren't anywhere else on her body, as he had assured himself many times. Sixteen years old, he told himself; what did he expect?

Well, he didn't expect her to be smiling.

"Chaim!" she greeted him happily. "O my passionate camel! We're all on our way to Kibbutz Kfar Yehuda, I'm going to be a kibbutznik, they promised I could clean the chicken coops, I'm crazy about chickens, we get paid the same as the men. Isn't it wonderful?"

"How much do the men get paid?"

"Nothing!"

"Why do you want to clean chicken coops for nothing? What's so wonderful about that?"

"We'll all be equal, men and women, girls and boys, I'll have as much right to tell the men what to do as they have to tell me. Think of it, I'll be able to tummel!"

"You always *enjoyed* doing whatever I told you to do!"

"Of course. But the girls from the kibbutz tell me I'll enjoy it more if you do what I tell you instead. And do it often. Don't expect me to carry the whole load any more. Also, I don't have to do it at all if I don't want to. Isn't that great?"

"Salome, listen." If he were going to teach Sonya a good lesson, Chaim knew he had to talk fast; the driver was starting up the bus. "It's a Jewish plot, you have a job to do for the PLO, climb out of the window, there's a motel over near Sodom, we'll get into a water bed, and I'll tell you a lot of military secrets!"

"Not right now, O my passionate camel," said Salome. "I have a splitting headache."

And she closed the window.

Not even Schoenbaum had fully realized the implications of

the Cabinet's decision. His purpose, as always, had been, foremost, Sonya's happiness. That the new law was only the beginning, that the Pinsker Street Cover-up would soon dwarf Watergate by its international dimensions, was beyond his immediate interest. When Sonya finally came out of the Lincoln bathroom, pinker but still pregnant, he had attempted to reason with her. This was no time for foolishness. A marriage, a child were at stake. Whatever Chaim-Harold's crimes, he had been the first to break. He had come to Sonya, repentant, and she had rebuffed him. She had called him momzer; he had not called her yenta. This indicated how great was his love. It was her turn to be forgiving.

Never, Sonya told him. Until Chaim-Harold came crawling to her, told her he had given up his belly dancer, and assured her she was Absolutely Right about everything. And that Horizontal was Beautiful.

Schoenbaum didn't press the matter further. He had an ace in the hole. Never underestimate the power of a Friend of Sophie's. The matter was in capable hands. The Lord had probably ghost-written that book Sonya was reading, which recommended Epsom salts and other similarly ineffective methods and thus protected all creatures great and small. God would figure Sonya out. Besides, Schoenbaum had no time for further argument. He had been told to come to Jerusalem for an urgent meeting with the Prime Minister.

There was a different atmosphere in Israel's government offices now. Where recently all had been gaiety, now there was an atmosphere of hard work. The slivovitz had been taken out of the water coolers; the secretaries' skirts had been lowered, and the necklines raised; brassieres had been installed. In the Jewish girls' new arrogance over the promulgations of the Eleventh Commandment as the law of the land, they had stopped wearing perfume, makeup, and jewelry, and any invitation to dinner had to be coupled with a financial statement.

Most ominous of all, there was happy whistling heard from behind the doors of the internal revenue department.

Schoenbaum had realized change was necessary; how much change, he was about to learn.

The returned Prime Minister had swung smoothly and powerfully back into his role as the head of state. He greeted Schoenbaum briefly from behind his desk, where he was seated in his customary open shirt, going over stacks of government papers. His attitude was very much that of a military commander in the heat of a campaign.

"Schoenbaum," he said, sliding a sheet of paper across his desk, "sign that right away, and let's get the show on the road."

"So what's this?" inquired the old man, slipping his rimless glasses onto his nose. He held the paper up to the light from the window.

"Don't bother to read, sign," snapped the Chief of State. "I'll tell you what it says later. We haven't got all day."

"Not so fast, sonny boy," said Schoenbaum, not in the least intimidated. "You think maybe you got here a greenhorn? I'll read, I'll think; then maybe I'll sign. From Schoenbaum nobody gets a blank check."

Still unable to read the fine print, he found a magnifying glass on the prime minister's desk, used for locating Israel on the world globe nearby. With the glass, he carefully studied the paper in his hand.

The Prime Minister sighed helplessly. "Here," he said, holding out his hand, "I'll read it to you."

Schoenbaum shook his head.

"Two things I learned from my old zayde," he said. "A, never sign what you don't read for yourself; B, never put anything in your wife's name. My zayde lived to be ninety-two because he couldn't read his doctor's prescriptions and never had them filled. His wife lived to be ninety-five and never got a nickel from his estate. A wise man, a saint."

"Read," groaned his opponent, "then sign. I haven't got all day."

"What's this?" inquired Schoenbaum, reading through the magnifying glass. "There never was an oil well on Pinsker Street?"

"It will help when we put back all the taxes," the Prime Minister explained. "We must make everyone believe there isn't any oil. That there never was. The Pinsker Street Cover-up. We're putting out a story to make the Arabs believe, to make our people believe, the whole thing didn't happen. It's the only way to save the nation. There never really was any oil in the first place. You made it all up."

"*Me?* So what was shooting by the sky from the well, shoe polish? What's in the tanks so it could pump through the pipes to the ships?"

"What well? What tanks? What ships?"

"By my place I bought from Uncle Zvi, twice what it's worth, a hundred wells they dug, everywhere is oil, did you see Haimowitz's Bass Weejuns?"

The Chief of State pressed a buzzer on his desk, and Shimon Gan immediately appeared, as if he had been waiting for the summons.

"Shimon, you're chief of intelligence?" his leader asked.

"Who else?"

"Was there ever any oil on Pinsker Street?"

"Pinsker Street? Don't make me laugh."

"Are we pumping our oil to ships in the harbor?"

"Of course not. Everyone knows Israel has no oil."

The Prime Minister turned to Schoenbaum. "You heard?" he inquired.

"Am I going crazy?" Schoenbaum asked.

"No," said the Chief. "You've been."

"Schoenbaum," interjected Shimon Gan before the old man could holler, "we have to tell everybody you're a little bit crazy, the Pinsker Street Gusher never happened, you imagined everything, that you're an old man, getting senile. Everybody will believe it.''

"Senile? *Schoenbaum?*" shouted Schoenbaum. "Play by me two games pinochle, I'll take from your teeth the inlays!''

"Shhh," remonstrated the prime minister, getting to his feet, agitated. "No one must hear. You must do this for Israel."

"Never. City Hall I'll fight till I drop dead!" He ran to the open window. "It's a lie!" he hollered to whoever happened to be listening. "By Pinsker Street is oil!''

Shimon Gan leaped to the window and shut it. The Premier's left eye had started twitching. He turned to his intelligence chief.

"Shimon," he whispered, "does the Secret Service still have some of those poisoned darts you got from the Mau Mau? And the blowguns?"

Shimon shook his head. "In Israel," he reminded the Prime Minister, "we don't operate that way. Besides, we need the old shlimazl's signature."

His Chief realized that, as usual, Schoenbaum had them over an oil barrel. He tried to reason as a last alternative.

"Schoenbaum," he said, "you know what has happened to the country. You know we agreed to try to turn things around. Golda even gave up the prime ministry. We are telling the whole world our oil was a bluff. The next meeting of the Knesset will be televised by satellite to the United States. It should get at least a fifty-four share; we're spotting it against a dramatization of Spiro Agnew's novel. I will tell the Knesset we bought our oil from Iran, through third parties so the Shah wouldn't realize what we were doing."

"You'll lie to the Knesset?"

"Of course. That's how they'll know we're back to normal. Then I'll explain we built a few oil tanks to hold the oil, pumped it back and forth through the pipes to look like more, and shipped it out a little at a time to different countries so they would think we had plenty. We started the whole conglomerate to hide the truth in the paperwork. Everyone will believe this; that's what conglomerates are for. I will say we did it to frighten the Arab heads of state to the peace table. When they shipped in the zoftik girls in the harems and the social fiber of Israel started to disintegrate, we realized the whole scheme could backfire, you should excuse the expression. All right? Now in order to make this plan work, we must destroy all the records. We've already blown up the Pinsker Street oil wells; now we'll cap them and build a synagogue on top. We'll—"

"Orthodox or Reformed?" Schoenbaum interrupted.

"We'll let *you* decide," beamed the Premier, seeing the first chink in the armor.

"In that case, should be by my property, the Sophie Schoenbaum Equal Opportunity Temple. Let the goyim fight each other; we should show them a united front. Orthodox and Reformed rabbis together in the same shul."

"You have a point," said the prime minister, holding out the agreement hopefully. "Sign."

"Not so fast, sonny boy. First I need it from you—"

"I know"—his opponent sighed—"in black and white on a piece paper. You'll have it."

"I'll wait," said Schoenbaum.

"We can't wait long. All of this must be done immediately, the wells capped, the records destroyed, so Israel can be broke and Jewish and impossible again."

"First, I have to talk to Chaim; he understands from the oil business."

"We've been trying to locate him; we haven't been able to find him," Shimon Gan, chief of intelligence, admitted. "We should never have closed down the Pillar of Salt Playboy Club; we used to know where everyone was."

"It's closed? No more naked shiksas?" Schoenbaum was all ears.

"No more," said the Prime Minister. "When the Knesset approved the Eleventh Commandment, the girls were sent to the kibbutzim. One week cleaning out the chicken coops, no one will *want* to shtup them. Our Jewish girls will be back on even terms.''

Schoenbaum started to smile. Carefully, he folded up the sheet of paper in his hands and placed it in the inside pocket of his blue serge suit.

"I'll take this home so I can read," he said. "For me you'll find Chaim Barak-Bernstein, send him to my house, he should apologize again to Sonya, tell her by him she is Absolutely Right. Buy him maybe a bunch flowers, roses, expensive. A box candy. Chocolate, the best. Champagne, French. If in the morning he's still by my house, in the Lincoln bed with Sonya, she's smiling, I'll sign.''

"You drive a hard bargain," said Shimon Gan, chief of intelligence, whose informants had kept him up to date on Chaim-Harold's activities. He knew how difficult it would be to get a Jewish Princess to smile under such circumstances, even if Chaim still had enough energy to make a proper apology.

"So if you can't, do me one favor. I'm an old man, but by me the lungs are still good.''

"What is it you want?" the Prime Minister asked, puzzled.

"From the Mau Mau," said Schoenbaum, "the blowgun and a few darts, Chaim shouldn't leave Sonya's bedroom.''

And he left, whistling loudly, his lungs obviously A number one.

Shemuhl Kishner, Shimon Gan's dedicated assistant, prowling Tel Aviv in his jeep, picked up Chaim-Harold Barak-Bernstein pounding on the door of the Ben Yehuda Street Bottomless, ignoring the "Closed by Eleventh Commandment" sign. Chaim was in a bad way; he had stopped off at the Waldorf-Astoria Bar and was now in the middle of a slivovitz crying jag. His world had collapsed; gone was his wife, probably also his child; gone were his office, his secretary, his oil, and the moons of his delight. Gone were all the houris in the luxurious seraglios on Dizengoff Street and Herzliya Pituach; gone to the kibbutzim. Although Chaim was not a very fastidious lover, he did have one firm rule: Never in a chicken coop. Salome might as well be back in high school in Juwara, even though she was shortly to convert to Judaism so that she would not be violating the new Commandment with the passionate camels on the kibbutz, who were passionate enough to ignore the chickens.

Chaim was brought to intelligence headquarters and given a cold shower and half an hour of oxygen inhalation, the standard antidote for slivovitz. Since Chaim had consumed an overdose, he was given a second cold shower. He was brought, still pale and weak, but very clean, before Shimon Gan. Aluf Gan explained to him that Chaim had been recalled to active service in the army; his first orders were to go back to Sonya once more and beg her forgiveness. The penalty for insubordination was summary execution. Chaim immediately became very sober and tried to dive out of the window. He was restrained by two lieutenants and hauled before General Gan once more.

Shimon explained the Schoenbaum Impasse to him, and appealed to his patriotism.

"You don't understand," Private Barak told the general. "First, Sonya will kill me. Second, if she doesn't, I'll kill myself. Third, if I don't, the army will kill me. We can all save time by letting me jump out the window."

"These offices are on the first floor," the general reminded him. "You wouldn't even get a mild concussion. But if you go back to Sonya and she throws you out, I promise you we'll let you up on the roof to jump."

Chaim was unconvinced, but finally, he realized more was at stake than his own life. Schoenbaum's signature was necessary for the Pinsker Street Cover-up to be successful. The world must be told there had been no oil, and the Israeli taxpayer must be returned to his customary state of insolvency, or the sabra spirit that had made the country great would disappear into the sloth and satiety of easy wealth and easy shiksas. This last argument was a mistake; sloth and satiety had been two of Chaim's lifetime ambitions.

But he suddenly realized he had grown up in the last few weeks. His undignified pursuit of Salome had been almost a reflex action, a result of frustration and anger. More than anything else, he needed Sonya and the unborn son she was threatening to erase. In addition to love, they symbolized his place in the continuity that was Israel; his son would be a link in a chain that stretched far into the past and a shaky distance into the future. The chain could have been destroyed by Salome; she had been an escape from the reality of his Jewish heritage, a lovely, soft, albeit pimpled escape; but now was a time for hard truth and a resolute turning to the unknown and unknowable tomorrow in which the Barak-Bernstein strain would continue undiluted in the land of his fathers. Whatever the sacrifice to his male chauvinism, he must go back to Sonya again and stop her before it was too late, even if he crawled all the way.

Chaim's clothes were cleaned and pressed, and intelligence supplied him, per Schoenbaum's instructions, with a bouquet, chrysanthemums instead of roses, Tel Aviv gumdrops instead of chocolate, and Carmel wine instead of French champagne. Israel had become Israel again, wise but poor.

With some trepidation, Chaim drove to the Savyon White House. As he pulled into the driveway, he saw Sonya in the rose garden. She had a shovel and was digging up large rocks, lifting them up in her hands and hurling them as far as she could, then bending down and digging again. Chapter Four of the *Liberated Woman's Guide*. Spectacular but unscientific. Possibility of successful results, less than one percent with babies, eighty-five percent with tulips. On the AMA's Maybe list. Sonya knew all this, but Chaim didn't. When she saw him out of the corner of her eye, she picked up the largest rock she could find and threw it, with an effort, as far as she could.

Then, with a loud, theatrical moan, she collapsed on the grass, clutching her middle.

Chaim was out of the Mercedes in a bound, leaped a rosebush, and rushed to her side. Wildly, he started to feel for her pulse. Anywhere. He was a doctor of oil, not of medicine.

"Momzer," she said, startled. "What are you feeling for?"

"Your pulse," Chaim said as he found it.

"Down there?" She was secretly pleased at his concern as well as his sense of direction, but she would never let him know. At least, not yet. "Nobody feels for a pulse down there!"

"Why not? You got a good beat there."

Sonya sat up and brushed his hand away, pretending anger. "How many times a night did you take your shiksa belly dancer's pulse?"

"Don't be such an old—" Chaim started to say, and then stopped. He remembered the briefing he had just received from psychological warfare. Don't call her a yenta; the fate of a nation is riding on you. "Don't be so stupid," he amended lamely. "And what were you doing, digging up rocks when you're pregnant?"

Sonya was on her feet now, adjusting her dress, regaining her regal rank of Jewish Princess.

"What do you think?" she said. "Hot Epsom salt baths just give me more headaches; I changed my method."

"You have no right!" Chaim shouted, the anger returning. "It's my baby, too! I want it to be born, I want to hold it in my two hands!"

"Like Mivka and Zivka?" Sonya inquired gently.

My God, thought Chaim. Rivka's Revenge. She told! What could he say? Again, his briefing from psychological warfare came to his assistance.

"You're Absolutely Right," Chaim said.

Sonya smiled inwardly. They were making progress. She turned away and started to pick up the shovel, but he kicked it away, as she hoped he would. The sky was starting to cloud over in the east, but she barely noticed.

"Sonya, I want you to know," Chaim admitted, "Rivka, Zivka, and Mivka were just to make you jealous."

"What about the Arab shiksa belly dancer? What names did you have for hers? Shakey and Fakey?"

"Fakey, never," Chaim assured her, a little of his anger returning, "Allah be praised."

"Go away," said Sonya, hoping he wouldn't. "Go away and never come back!" She walked away from him and sneaked a look to see if he was following. He wasn't. She stopped.

"Sonya," he said, "don't run away. It won't do any good. Remember how the earth moved for us?"

"The cesspool," Sonya reminded him, "or maybe Dimona. That was all."

"I'm not so sure anymore," he told her. "I'm beginning to believe we were meant for each other. That it's written in the stars."

Sonya laughed. She meant it to sound derisive. She couldn't let him know she was touched.

"Sing it for me, Chaim," she said.

"Don't laugh." He crossed to her now and took her hands in his. It was his own idea, not psychological warfare's. "In the caves above En Feshkha," he told her, and he was almost whispering now, "I heard a Voice. It spoke to me. It told me where to find the cholent pot with the scroll, the Eleventh Commandment."

"So?" The clouds were growing heavier now, more menacing. But still Sonya didn't notice.

"I tell you I heard the Voice of God, all you can say is, 'So?' "

"I'm not very religious, at my cousin Moishe's bar mitzvah, thirteen years old, he tried to feel me up."

"All he was trying to say was, 'Today I am a man.' "

"*That* he had written in his speech. The feeling up was an ad lib."

"Sonya, we're getting off the subject! When I heard His voice in the cave—"

"*His* voice? How can you be sure God isn't a woman?"

"Because He never talks unless He has something to say!"

Sonya turned away, angrily, and crossed to sit down on a bench among the roses in the White House rose garden. Chaim followed and, remembering the chrysanthemums, handed her the bouquet.

"What's this?" she inquired.

"The army thought I should give you a bouquet."

"Cheap chrysanthemums? When we have all these roses?"

"The Army is new at bouquets. But I want to tell you something. Even if they had issued me orchids, they wouldn't be half as beautiful as you are right now." Again, Psychological Warfare had warned him against being too sentimental. But here, in the fading afternoon light, a single beam of sunlight streaking Sonya's hair through a tiny hole in the clouds, as if by heavenly command—and who would bet against that?— Sonya looked like the Sonya Chaim had fallen in love with at Ben-Gurion Airport. Anger and excitement and hope had turned her cheeks the color of Salome's, without the necessity for ocher. He wanted to fold her in his arms and have everything the way it used to be, when their love was new and each kiss an inspiration, as in the old-fashioned song.

Stardust in Tel Aviv, who would have believed it?

Sonya's eyes flashed as she looked at her former lover and present momzer—dangerous eyes, eyes worth conquering, unlike the soft and yielding eyes of the acquiescent Arabian houris. Chaim looked into Sonya's eyes and longed for Salome again. After all, there is a time for danger, but when you are in the frantic condition Chaim had been in ever since he had felt Sonya's lovely pulse, acquiescence has a lot going for it.

"I'm prettier than those Arab-shiksa-nafka-belly-dancers," Sonya declared. "Even pregnant." Chaim's early-warning system went into action. There was something feminine in Sonya's voice that hadn't been there before. She was finally lowering the mask, telling him that perhaps it had been pretense, his case wasn't hopeless, in spite of all the things she had said and done. But the ultimate decision was still in doubt. Chaim would have to win her again, fairly and squarely. Sonya was nobody's pushover.

Anymore.

"You're Absolutely Right," Chaim whispered, and the Princess smiled. At the window of the Oval Office, Chaim caught a glimpse of Schoenbaum peering through the curtains. As Sonya stood up, the beam of sunlight through the cloud seemed to follow her. Chaim had a feeling they were being watched by a Celestial Voyeur.

"Let me explain why it won't do any good for you to keep digging rocks in the garden," Chaim continued, "and why hot Epsom salt baths only gave you headaches. The Voice promised your father you would have his grandchild, for Sophie's sake. So you could dig forever, you could go to the clinic, you could even eat Mexican food, you are still going to have my son."

He put his arms around her and tried to kiss her, but Sonya pulled away from him. As with all true love, the course of this one wasn't smooth. Chaim had just touched a sensitive nerve.

"It's my body and my right," she insisted. "If I don't want to have a son, I don't have to!"

"Don't be so sure," Chaim said, his nerve as sensitive as hers. "I don't think God believes in women's lib. Remember, He once had a son by remote control!"

Sonya started to laugh. "Oh, come on, Chaim," she said. "You know as well as I that the Bible is a fairy tale."

The spotlight on her head suddenly seemed to be snuffed out as the hole in the cloud closed, almost as if the Projectionist had become angry. There was a rumbling in the east, but Sonya took no notice. She had Chaim on the defensive again, the Princess was back on the throne, she wanted to make him crawl a little before unfrogging him. Hastily, she picked up the shovel and started to dig up the biggest rock she could find before Chaim could stop her.

There was a flash of lightning followed by a tremendous clap of thunder. The sky above the Savyon White House was illuminated by the flaming words:

THOU WILT NAME HIM JACOB

As the words disappeared, there was another violent lightning bolt:

SOPHIE SAYS

Sonya dropped the shovel. She stared at the sky, trembling, as Chaim put his arms around her again.

"This is one City Hall even Schoenbaum can't fight," he told her. "You have to give me another chance. A child should have a father."

He kissed her.

"You'll stay home?" Sonya wanted to know.

"One night out for pinochle," Chaim said, kissing her again, but determined to maintain his manly independence.

"You don't play pinochle," Sonya reminded him.

"I'll learn. From your father. But I figure, with all the belly dancers cleaning chicken coops, it will be the only reason to get out of the house in Israel from now on."

"Thank God," said Sonya, "for the Eleventh Commandment." She kissed him. "Listen," Sonya said, "it was terrible for me to pretend I was trying to lose our son. I was just getting even, like you were getting even with Salome. Of course, not as often."

"Sonya, look," Chaim said, "I came today because the army made me, but I would have come anyway, as soon as I got the courage. I love you. I married you. But I didn't realize I'd have to be a dull Jewish husband with a Jewish Princess wife in order to preserve the race. Still, if the only way for Israel to continue to exist is for me to forget about shiksas, I'm a soldier, I'll force myself."

Sonya started to laugh once more.

"Chaim," she said, "whom do you think you married? The Jewish Shirley Temple? Believe me, I was very friendly with a few shaygitzes, back in New York, before I met you. But I had all the pressures to get married, from my father, my mother. When I finally did it, I thought the only way to make it work was to be like all the others: Holler, nag, horizontal. It didn't work. It never really works. But I want to make you a promise. On the nights when there's no pinochle, we'll play Sodom and Gomorrah."

It was starting to rain now, a soft gentle rain. For a moment they stood in a warm embrace, letting the raindrops enfold them, and then Chaim picked up Sonya in his arms.

"Let's go to the Lincoln Bedroom," he whispered in her ear. "I'll get a deck of cards."

He started to run with her toward the White House.

"Not so fast, you must be careful of our son!" Sonya whispered.

"You're Absolutely Right," said Chaim, and kissed her again.

Inside the Oval Office, Schoenbaum had watched the entire tableau. Now he turned and crossed to the desk, an exact replica of the one Franklin D. Roosevelt had used, and sank into the swivel chair behind it, an exact replica of the one that had been built for John F. Kennedy. From a box he took a Manuelo y Vega cigar, an exact replica of the one designed for Fidel Castro, and lit it, letting the powerful smoke rise to the ceiling.

"Jacob," mused Schoenbaum, happily, "a nice name."

The General Assembly of the United Nations, gathered in special session in New York City, listened carefully as Henry Kissinger made his report.

"The political and economic balance of the world has been restored to equilibrium because of Israel's overpowering adherence to the tradition of the Mosiac Law and its unwritten Eleventh Commandment," he declared. "The world can never thank this little nation enough for its unselfish sacrifice and unprecedented retreat from a position of economic power that might have strangled the entire Arab community of nations, as well as Europe and the United States. To little Israel, on behalf of President Jimmy Carter, I have been authorized to say 'mazel tov.' "

He stepped down, to thunderous applause.

Next, the British ambassador echoed Kissinger's words, thanking the little country for saving the massive but impoverished British Empire that, through the Balfour Declaration, had been responsible for the establishment of a Jewish homeland in Palestine. He considered the debt repaid.

The French ambassador to the United Nations also gave Israel his thanks for not having used its momentary economic power to punish France for a few small, unintentional slights. They could expect that La Belle France, in the future, would continue to be the same La Belle France Israel had grown to know and love.

The Pope had sent an emissary to announce that his arthritis was better. He was saying three Hail Marys for Jacob Schoenbaum.

The General Assembly then swung into action.

By a vote of 110 to 0, with 14 abstentions, 11 calling in sick, and 9 stuck in traffic without gas, Israel was ordered to give back the Golan Heights, the Sinai Desert, the West Bank of the Jordan, all Jerusalem, and a belly dancer named Salome, for whom the sultan of Oman had prepared four large cushions and some butter.

All captured terrorists were to be released and given back their weapons, fully loaded, with the safety catches filed down.

An invitation was sent to Yasir Arafat to return and make another speech. He didn't have to shave.

Israel was to be expelled from the United Nations.

God was in His heaven—all was right with the world.

Glossary of Foreign Terms

Agora One agora is one hundredth of an Israeli pound. The Israeli pound used to be one-third of the American dollar. As of this writing, it is about one-eighth and falling. This makes the agora worth about one-tenth of one cent, which in the boisterous Carmel Market of Tel Aviv will buy you nothing but contempt. In biblical times Judas sold Jesus for thirty drachmas, or just three hundred agorot, which gives you an indication of what inflation has done to the price of Gentiles.

Aleph The first letter of the Hebrew alphabet, also used as the number 1. It was the Arabs who invented the idea of representing numbers by separate symbols instead of the more economical method of doubling over the letters of the alphabet. The Hebrews could never adopt an Arabic improvement; therefore, even today the Hebrew multiplication table is, to many, indistinguishable from the Song of Solomon, which causes some confusion.

Alter Kocker An old man. A querulous, quarrelsome, ineffectual old man. A male yenta. The literal translation is exactly what you thought it was, and you won't get any further explanation here. Among the cognoscenti, it is often abbreviated to AK.

Aluf, rov aluf A high rank in the Israeli army, roughly corresponding to an American general. Roughly, because in the Israeli army, an aluf is supposed to lead his men in battle, not direct them from a bunker in the rear. Thus, if he is unpopular, he runs the risk of being shot at from two directions simultaneously, which has been found to promote efficiency. A sgan aluf is a lieutenant general, who usually enters battle just in front of an aluf, so the rank is not much sought after.

Brucha A blessing, a prayer of thanksgiving. An Orthodox Jew during a single day may pronounce as many as one or two hundred bruchas, for such various joys as inheriting a million dollars or going to bed with a beautiful woman or upon receiving bad news. The bad news is usually that the beautiful woman has spent his million dollars and has given him a social disease. Some days it's hardly worthwhile to get out of bed, no matter whose. This also calls for a brucha.

Catskills The mountains near New York City where Rip Van Winkle slept for twenty years. In modern days, a succession of kosher resort hotels, hip to thigh, ruled over by an army of social directors, who would lose their jobs if a guest was allowed to sleep for more than twenty minutes. Any Jewish maiden who spends two weeks in the Catskills and returns intact is considered an untouchable.

Cholent Jewish pot roast designed for the Sabbath. Since cooking on the Holy Day is not allowed, the meat is put into the oven the day before, where it is allowed to rest. If you don't take it out for twenty-four or twenty-six hours and it happens to have cooked itself, the sin belongs to the pot roast, not the cook.

Chumsin The wind out of the Sahara that regularly roasts the Holy Land, making life so unbearable the PLO often takes credit for it.

Chutzpah Nerve, gall, effrontery. So many jokes have been made about it, no one would have the chutzpah to add another.

Farkockta Cursed. Terrible. Stupid. The degree depends on the vehemence with which the word is pronounced. Its origin is obvious and unprintable, at least here.

Geshrei A holler, a yell, usually in the form of the word "gevalt." Leo Rosten, in *The Joys of Yiddish,* tells of the Countess de Rothschild, in the throes of labor pains upstairs in the baronial manor while her nervous husband played cards with the doctor downstairs.

Came the shrill cry of the countess, *"Mon Dieu! Mon Dieu!"* The husband leaped up, but the doctor said there was plenty of time. They played on.

Soon the countess screamed, "Oh, God, oh, *God!"* Up leaped the haggard husband.

"No," said the doctor. "Not yet. Deal." The husband dealt. . . . They played on.

Came a geshrei from upstairs, "Ge-*valt!"* Up rose the obstetrician. "Now."

Kibbutz A Jewish communal farm or community. Each individual gives up all his worldly belongings when entering, and after that it is share and share alike. Many kibbutzim have been established on the controversial borders with Lebanon, Egypt, Jordan, and Syria. Since each kibbutznik has an equal stake in the kibbutz, when war breaks out—as it inevitably does—he fights with a certain personal involvement. It is similar to the story of the Jewish private in World War II who was about to be court-martialed for insubordination when he turned up at a ceremony to receive the Congressional Medal of Honor. When Eisenhower asked his commander how this miraculous change had been brought about, the commander said, "Sir, I gave him a jeep and a machine gun and told him he was in business for himself."

L'chayim Literally, "To life," the toast made when raising the glass before drinking. In the case of slivovitz, it is more of a prayer than a toast.

Manuelo y Vega A Havana cigar, known for its flavor, aroma, and price, all of them deserving of the adjective "farkockta." It is rumored King Mithridates had a cigar taster who smoked his Manuelo y Vegas for him. Mithridates, he died old.

Mikvah The religious bath taken by Jewish women before the wedding night, after the birth of a child, and after the menstrual period. An Orthodox wife is not supposed to have sexual relations with her husband until seven days after taking the mikvah, although an attempt has been made by Orthodox men to shorten the waiting period by the installation of a Jacuzzi.

Meshuggener An insane person, or one who doesn't agree with you.

Mitzvah   The equivalent of a Boy Scout's Good Deed, However, since one of the mitzvahs a Jewish male can perform is to be fruitful and multiply, it seems likely to be reserved for Eagle Scouts.

Momzer   A bastard. Under Hebrew law, an illegitimate child inherits from the father; therefore, when a rich man is involved, the mother often calls her child a momzer as a term of endearment.

Mohel   The rabbi who performs the ritual circumcision on newly born male children. Since the child's anatomy, at that age, is minuscule, the job requires a steady hand, a sharp knife, and a sense of proportion. A mohel is not allowed to drink the ceremonial slivovitz until after the operation; otherwise, the Lord's admonition to be fruitful and multiply might be cut off in midsentence.

Nafka   A prostitute. Most Jewish men will not admit there can be such a shameful thing as a Jewish nafka. Even if a prostitute should start to sing "Hatikvah" during the act, a Jewish man will insist she must be a shiksa who overheard it while practicing her trade in the basement of Temple Emanuel. Considerably impressed, he will often ask for an encore.

Nebbish   A Haimowitz. Or if you insist, a nonentity, a person so unsure of himself he considers it an honor to be mistaken for a shlemiel.

Neturey Karta   Literally, "The keepers of the books." This refers to the Orthodox religious sect that has appointed itself the true interpreters of the Old Testament. It is this sect that proclaims that joy is sinful and, therefore, there must be no bodily contact during the sexual act. For this reason a sheet must be thrown over the body of the woman. Luckily for the preservation of the race, it is allowed to have one hole in it, but the couple must think only religious thoughts. This is possible because, luckily, there are some sections of the Bible that are pretty dirty.

Nudnik   A nuisance, a pest. A nudnik has been described as a man whose purpose in life is to bore the rest of humanity, and succeeds.

Oy   The most expressive word in the Yiddish language, normally employed to express dismay. When spoken in duplicate, such as, "Oy oy!" it is sometimes so powerful as to provoke tears. It must be used sparingly. Only when an unmarried Jewish girl is informed she is about to have triplets is the ultimate form allowed, "Oy oy *oy!*"

Payess   The unshorn, braided sideburns worn by Orthodox Jews. They are supposed to symbolize the unharvested corners of the fields left to be gleaned by widows and orphans, according to the Bible. On the other hand, it is rumored that the style came into fashion when a member of the Neturey Karta fell in love with Rebecca of Sunnybrook Farm.

Pupik   Literally, the belly button, but often expanded to mean various adjoining anatomical areas. For a girl to expose her pupik is considered uncouth. Habitual pupik flashers are subject to excommunication and extreme popularity.

Rosh Hashonah   The Jewish New Year, celebrated by the blowing of the ram's horn to call the faithful to prayer in the temple. To make certain that even the least religious will show up, the temple is filled with honey cake, wine, and chopped herring. The ancient Hebrew melody played on the ram's horn is actually Moses' Mess Call.

Shabbas or Shabbat   Shabbas is the Yiddish word for the Sabbath, Saturday. Shabbat is the Hebrew word, employed in Israel. The Orthodox will perform no work on the Sabbath, and work has a wide definition. In the Orthodox Deborah Hotel in Tel Aviv, the staff tears up the toilet paper for the guests on Friday; what is done with the torn paper on Saturday is a matter of conscience. Why there is the discrepancy between the Hebrew and the Christian Sabbath days is unknown. The Bible states clearly the Lord worked six days and rested on the seventh; how that could be interpreted as Saturday in one religion and Sunday in another is what makes horse races.

Shaygitz   Any young boy or young man who is not of the Jewish faith. If a Jewish girl goes out with a shaygitz, her mother will immediately drop dead. This, at least, is the threat, although in actual practice the mother usually limits her reaction to a small heart attack. If the shaygitz has a rich father, a severe headache sometimes suffices.

Shiksa   A Gentile girl. The implication is that all shiksas are beautiful, slender, and afflicted with constant nymphomania. Therefore, much of a Jewish boy's life is often given over to a constant search for truth.

Shlemiel   A fool, a bumbler, a man with ten thumbs. It is axiomatic that if a shlemiel were to be seduced by the most beautiful woman in the world, her zipper would get stuck and he wouldn't be able to open it.

Shlimazl   A born loser. Much lower in the scale than a Shlemiel. If a shlimazl were seduced by the most beautiful woman in the world, *his* zipper would get stuck, and *she* wouldn't be able to open it.

Shmatta   A rag, an old piece of fabric, a cheap dress or suit. But the term can be relative. If a shlimazl has an expensive tuxedo tailored exactly to his measure by the finest tailors at Saks Fifth Avenue, on him it will look like a shmatta.

Shmuck   Unfortunately, the literal translation is the most apt: a prick. For some reason, the word *Schmuck* in German means "jewelry," which gives some insight into the German character. However, used by the Lord, it can be considered His general word for all humanity; in the light of all we have put Him through, only a shmuck would disagree with Him.

Shtup   The sexual act, you should excuse the expression. However, the word connotes enjoyment; one rarely shtups one's wife.

Shul   A Jewish house of worship; actually, a way of life. Before each shul is built, the battle between Orthodox and Reformed Jewry occurs. The story is told of the shipwrecked Jewish sailor who is rescued from a tiny desert island by a merchant ship. As they leave, he shows them the stone temple he has constructed with his bare hands during the time he was cast away, and the captain of the ship marvels at its size and beauty. As they round the tip of the island, they see another building, equally large, equally beautiful, obviously build by the same hands. "What is that?" the captain asks, puzzled. "That," says the ragged sailor, with considerable vehemence, "is the shul I wouldn't be caught dead in."

Yenta   An old gossip, a complainer. A young girl is called a maidl until she is either pregnant or married, preferably not in that order. A yenta can be married and the mother of eight, even her husband will not admit to having had anything to do with her. It is assumed that the Virgin Mary was a yenta.